Essential Whitman

The ESSENTIAL POETS Series

Essential
Whitman

Selected and with an Introduction
by Galway Kinnell

HarperCollins books may be purchased for educational,
business, or sales promotional use. For information,
please write: Special Markets Department, HarperCollins
Publishers, 10 East 53rd Street, New York, NY 10022.

Photograph of Whitman by G. Frank E. Pearsall, 1872.
Reproduced by permission of the National Portrait
Gallery, Smithsonian Institute, Washington, D.C.; Gift of
Mr. and Mrs. Feinberg.

Designed by Nicola Ferguson

Printed on acid-free paper

Library of Congress Cataloging-in-Publication Data is
available upon request.

ISBN-10: 0-06-088792-3
ISBN-13: 978-0-06-088792-6

10 11 12 13 DIX/RRD 10 9 8 7 6 5 4

CONTENTS

FOREWORD

I HAVE ALWAYS BELIEVED that there is an untapped poetry audience, readers who are just waiting for the kiss of verse to awaken them into a landscape of emotion and image they've never experienced. Contrary to the common cliché, poetry is not actually difficult to understand, on at least one of the many levels a poem may work on—often just the simple, literary level of what the words are saying and what they invoke—"simple truth miscalled simplicity," wrote Shakespeare. Poetry has, and will always, play an important part in our lives. It's obvious to most that during the critical moments in our lives—that would include all rites of passage, from birth, through marriage, to tragedy and death—poetry surfaces to express our deepest feelings, elicits in us a wholeness and depth. A kind of shorthand of the emotions and the soul, a pure form of expression and experience.

So Ecco took it upon itself to go to the keepers of

the flame—they would be the most accomplished poets still living and practicing the art—to pick what is most essential from the canon that has been passed down to us. Thus began Ecco's ESSENTIAL POETS.

It's appropriate that we now celebrate our thirty-fifth anniversary with the reissue of this series, re-packaged but unscathed—a fresh format for the canon's ongoing journey into the hands and hearts of the new readers who will discover the magic in the distillation of this language they inherit. The music of the verbal object.

DANIEL HALPERN
Publisher
Ecco
An Imprint of HarperCollins*Publishers*

INTRODUCTION

THE POEMS of Walt Whitman meant little to me when I read them in high school and college. Luckily, when I was teaching at the University of Grenoble in my late twenties, I was required to give a course on Whitman. My experience of his work then was intense, the more so because, in a foreign country, it was my one real connection to my own language. Soon I understood that poetry could be transcendent, hymnlike, a cosmic song, and yet remain idolatrously attached to the creatures and things of our world. Under Whitman's spell I stopped writing in rhyme and meter and in rectangular stanzas and turned to long-lined, loosely cadenced verse; and at once I felt immensely liberated. Once again, as when I first began writing, it seemed it might be possible to say everything in poetry. Whitman has been my principal master ever since.

So the choice of poems for *Essential Whitman* came naturally. I simply made a list of the poems I like best. I discovered that my list included the poems generally thought to be Whitman's greatest and that it represented the major aspects of his poetic talent. My selection did not differ much from the selection most modern editors would make. Only "The Runner" and "Sparkles from the Wheel" might be considered idiosyncratic choices. Wonderful poems were left out, but in such a book, this is as it must be; nor, regrettably, was there room for the lecture-essay, "An American Primer" or selections from *Specimen Days*.

Once I had settled upon which poems to use, all that remained to do was to choose the versions. This proved to be more difficult. *Leaves of Grass* came out in six editions. Each time Whitman added new poems, enlarging the book from twelve poems in 1855 to 383 in 1892. He also revised the poems already present. Many of the revisions could be called fine tuning, but quite a number went to the very heart of the poems. A poem called "Great Are the Myths" in successive editions was revised, lengthened, shortened, and at last dropped. Whitman took passages from one poem and put them in another. He made several poems of one poem, one poem of several. "Song of Myself" did not reach final form until twenty-six years after first publication.

Normally, of course, an editor would present the poems in the versions the author considered final. And indeed, some of Whitman's changes improve the poems in important ways. His deletions, in particular, are often well taken and sometimes make a decisive difference. Here, for example, are three lines from the 1855 version of "Song of Myself":

> *Swiftly arose and spread around me the peace and joy*
> *and knowledge that pass all the art and argument of*
> *the earth;*
> *And I know that the hand of God is the elderhand of*
> *my own,*
> *And I know that the spirit of God is the eldest brother of*
> *my own*

Here are the lines again as they appear in 1881:

> *Swiftly arose and spread around me the peace and*
> *knowledge that pass all the argument of the earth,*
> *And I know that the hand of God is the promise of*
> *my own,*
> *And I know that the spirit of God is the brother of*
> *my own*

The substitution of "promise" for "elderhand" in the second line is, to me, an error, but the deletions in the first and third lines are brilliant. In the first instance, taking away a few nouns transforms one of Whitman's most cluttered lines into one of his most flowing and moving. When the unnecessary adjective is stricken from the third line, it, too, suddenly shines.

Not only deletions, but rewritings as well, occa-

sionally improve the poems. How much more im-
mediate "Crossing Brooklyn Ferry" became after
Whitman rewrote the first line,

Flood-tide of the river, flow on! I watch you face to face,

to read:

Flood-tide below me! I see you face to face!

The 1856 line, "I too lived,"—weakened by the 1860
revision, "I too lived, (I was of old Brooklyn),"—came
to perfection in 1867: "I too lived, Brooklyn of
ample hills was mine."

If most of the changes were as good as these, the
question of which version to use would not arise. An
editor would simply reprint the poems as Whitman
left them. But most readers who look closely at Whit-
man's revisions soon realize that while some may
help, most do not, and many harm the poems, often
severely. Whitman may be poetry's most spectacular
victim of the law of elapsed time.

All writers know this law: revision succeeds in in-
verse ratio to the amount of time passed since the
work was written. Revision is most likely to improve
a poem when it directly follows composition, be-
cause it is, in fact, a slower, more reflective phase of
the creative act. It is most likely to fail if many years
have passed—such as the quarter century between
the first publication and the last revision of *Leaves of*

Grass. The only exception to the law is that ill-written and extraneous material may be excised with good effect at any time.

One reason why delayed revision often fails is that the writer eventually loses track of what he or she was originally trying to do—or more likely, was doing without trying. Great works are often written more by exploration, by feel, by instinct, than by fixed intention; and so it is easy for an author to forget the reasons—if he or she ever articulated them—for those inspired leaps, those sudden decisions and shifts of direction, which were vivid and compelling during composition. When Socrates questioned the poets of Athens, he discovered they wrote not by reason but by inspiration or madness and could not tell him what their poems meant. Certainly it was in an inspired, mad, illuminated state that Walt Whitman wrote the first version of *Leaves of Grass.* Sure enough, as Malcolm Cowley shows in the introduction to his reissue of the 1855 *Leaves of Grass,* before long Whitman forgot the original intent of his poem.

In particular, he forgot that the poem which was to become known as "Song of Myself" was not about himself, Walter Whitman, but about a representative man, a workman-poet, "Walt Whitman, an American, one of the roughs, a kosmos," as he describes himself in the 1855 edition, a person, furthermore, who was "not merely of the New World but of Africa Europe or Asia—a wandering savage." With each revision the poem became less representative and more exclusively autobiographical. In 1867 he changed the above description of the author to read, "Walt Whitman am I, of mighty Manhattan the son," and dropped the part about belonging to other continents. In 1881 he added this passage, suggesting that the protagonist is literally himself:

> *My tongue, every atom of my blood, form'd from this*
> *   soil, this air,*
> *Born here of parents born here from parents the same,*
> *   and their parents the same,*
> *I, now thirty-seven years old in perfect health begin,*
> *Hoping to cease not till death.*

In 1860 Whitman scrapped the 1856 title, "A Poem of Walt Whitman, an American," which makes clear the representative character of the poet-hero, and in 1881 he called it, "Song of Myself," a title which allows one to think the poem is about the actual author.

Another reason for the law of elapsed time is that the poet who revises belatedly may no longer be exactly the same person who composed. Certainly Whitman was not. As the Good Gray Poet (a mantle he put on in the late 1860s), he had lost some of his youthful arrogance, intransigence, and extraordinary shamelessness. Perhaps, too, he had been chastened by Emerson's new aloofness, by mocking reviews, by the realization that over the years he was acquiring notoriety but not readers. He began to excise from poems things he had once blurted out that could expose him to ridicule. From "Crossing the Brooklyn Ferry," for example, he removed a reference to himself as a "solitary committer" (whatever that is, but it sounds awful) and he dropped some brilliant but revealing passages from "The Sleepers," including this mysterious evocation of adolescent experience:

I feel ashamed to go naked about the world.
I am curious to know where my feet stand—and what
*   is this flooding me, childhood or manhood—and*
*   the hunger that crosses the bridge between.*

The cloth laps a first sweet eating and drinking,
Laps life-swelling yolks—laps ear of rose-corn, milky
*   and just ripened;*
The white teeth stay, and the boss-tooth advances
*   in darkness,*
And liquor is spilled on lips and bosoms by touching
*   glasses, and the best liquor afterward.*

He also dropped this tortured denunciation of his father:

Now Lucifer was not dead—or if he was I am his
*   sorrowful terrible heir,*

I have been wronged—I am oppressed—I hate him
  that oppresses me,
I will either destroy him, or he shall release me.

Damn him! how he does defile me,
How he informs against my brother and sister and takes
  pay for their blood,
How he laughs when I look down the bend after the
  steamboat that carries away my woman.

Now the vast dusk bulk that is the whale's bulk, it
  seems mine,
Warily, sportsman! though I lie so sleepy and sluggish,
  my tap is death.

The man who once said, "Unscrew the locks from the doors! Unscrew the doors themselves from their jambs!" apparently had second thoughts and wanted to screw the locks and doors back on again.

This self-protective, perhaps somewhat self-important new Whitman took on a more conventional poetic style as well. "Song of Myself" had started out to be a "language experiment": mixing the plain names of things, the great basic words, popular locutions, slang, technical terminology, disappeared words, Whitman proposed a new language for American poetry, contemporary, vivid, muscular, and at the same time fantastic, musical, and self-generating. But by the mid-sixties his work began to fill up with the very poeticisms and archaisms he had started off by excluding — "o'er," "e'en," "erewhile," "i'," "'tis," "ope," and many more.* Whitman changed "listen" to "list" and eventually went so far as to title a poem, "On, on the Same, ye Jocund Twain!"

Many of Whitman's revisions seem intended to domesticate the "barbaric yawp" and make his verse sound more recognizably like poetry. He inverted word order: "Now I stand on this spot," became, "Now on this spot I stand"; "Out of the rocked cradle," turned into, "Out of the cradle endlessly rocking." Whitman went back over the whole text of *Leaves* and changed the preterite and past participle "ed" to "'d" so that, on the page, in this respect at least, his work would look like the poetry of the past. He threw in more and more foreign words, sometimes with comic effect: "No dainty dulce affettuoso I!" His old, bold way of setting simple declarative sentences side by side must have struck him now as inelegant, and he subordinated one to the other: "He turns his quid of tobacco, his eyes get blurred with the manuscript," became, "He turns his quid of tobacco while his eyes blur with the manuscript."

He became less trustful of the common instinct that makes language intelligible and felt it necessary to explain perfectly comprehensible, spontaneous

---

*For a fuller discussion and more illustrations, see Roger Asselineau, *The Evolution of Walt Whitman,* vol. II of *The Creation of a Book* (Cambridge, Mass.: Harvard University Press, 1962).

turns of phrase: "Sleeps at my side all night and close on the peep of the day," became, "Sleeps at my side through the night, and withdraws at the peep of the day with stealthy tread," and, "The suns I see and the suns I do not see," turned into the mostly redundant: "The bright suns I see and the dark suns I cannot see." Slightly odd constructions he conventionalized: "The worst suffering and restless," became, "The worst suffering and the most restless." He revised straightforward phrases to make them more literary and deleted some of his happiest, but unliterary, touches. The word that had to disappear from this line, "Where the laughing-gull scoots by the slappy shore and laughs her near-human laugh," is, of course, "slappy." And this wonderfully wacko line, "Washes and razors for foofoos—for me freckles and a bristling beard," he dropped entirely.

These examples of Whitman's destructive changes illustrate the hard choices facing an editor. The sad truth is that the final edition of *Leaves of Grass* is far less exciting than the first. Some of the great poems are muddy from too much tampering. Wonderful passages are missing. The original daring and verbal brilliance had been compromised. "Song of Myself" has changed its very character. Much as I believe in respecting a poet's own final judgment about his poems, I found it too painful to present *Leaves of Grass* in this form.

The obvious alternative, to follow Malcolm Cowley and give the poems in their original, most energetic versions, was very appealing. The drawback was that to do so would mean ignoring those occasional brilliant rewritings that Whitman came up with, and leaving in place dull and superfluous lines that Whitman wisely struck out.

I puzzled long and hard over the dilemma—to use the latest versions and get some of the great poems in inferior form, or to present the earliest versions and do without the best of the revisions.

I came up with this solution. I took as my starting point what I regard as the most satisfactory version of each poem (usually, but not always, the earliest version). I then compared it with all other versions. When I found a distinctly superior reading—some happy rewriting or blessed deletion, or in the case of superseded versions, an abandoned felicity—I incorporated it into the version at hand. Some of the poems in this book, therefore, are in versions that have never existed before.

No doubt some readers will object to this procedure. They will not be mollified by knowing that the incorporations from other versions are rather few and that all of them are indicated in the notes. I understand the objection. My only justification is the hope that, unorthodox as it is, the method has made it possible to present Whitman's poetry at its best. And I know this method makes the book unsuitable for readers who, for whatever reason, need an intact version. Happily for them—and indeed for all who would judge the quality of Whitman's revisions for themselves—the editions of 1855, 1860, and 1881 are in print.

In punctuation I have usually followed the practice of the 1860 edition for poems published up to that time: dashes and commas, rather than a series of dots, to indicate caesuras; aversion to the exclamation point and semicolon; and a weakness for hyphenation. In later poems I have used the punctuation of the 1881 edition, except that I have kept all the original dashes and many of the discarded commas.

The first three editions of *Leaves of Grass* did not have numbered sections. In the fourth and fifth editions Whitman went back and divided some of the longer poems into sections. The section divisions are so useful that I have put them into even the early, unsectioned versions. The reader will know a version did not have sections to begin with when the section numbers appear on the left-hand margin; and that they originally did have sections when the numbers are centered, in larger typeface, above the sections.

As for titles, it would have been simple to use the familiar ones in the 1881 edition. In the case of four poems, however, I chose earlier titles. With one, I had no alternative. The later title, "I Sing the Body Electric," is the first line of the poem, but in the version used here ("Poem of the Body") it does not appear at all.

My choice of titles for the other three was more

a matter of judgment. The 1860 title, "Sleep-Chasings," is more apt than "The Sleepers," since only a part of this poem concerns sleepers, whereas all of it can be characterized as "sleep-chasings." The 1856 title, "Poem of the Proposition of Nakedness," has the no-nonsense, let's-just-describe-the-poem quality of all the early titles, and I find it more satisfactory than the catchier, "Respondez!" "Elemental Drifts" is a title too beautiful in itself to exchange for "As I Ebbed with the Ocean of Life."

I kept the title "Song of Myself" even though it may not be quite as accurate as the earlier, "A Poem of Walt Whitman, an American." This latter I have appended as a subtitle, hoping it will discourage a narrowly autobiographical reading.

A word about "Once I Passed Through a Populous City," which appears here in the manuscript version. As published, the poem describes an encounter with a woman, but in this version, the encounter is with a man. To fit the poem in the "Enfans d'Adam" poems, that section of *Leaves of Grass* about love between a man and a woman, Whitman changed the man to a woman and deleted both the poignant "we wandered" and, what is so precious and so seldom found in love poems, the evocation of the actual other — "one rude and ignorant man." I find the manuscript version stronger by far.

Whitman spent the last part of his life trying to get his book right. He kept working over those old poems, as Lady Gregory said of Yeats, as if he were in competition for eternity. As Whitman grew older, not only did his creative powers wane but his critical faculties became erratic, and he was never able to achieve that last goal and make a perfect *Leaves of Grass*. On the contrary, the more he searched for perfection, the further away it went. A year before his death, Whitman said, "In the long run the world will do what it pleases with the book." I would like to interpret this remark as indicating acceptance of such enterprises as this attempt of mine to consolidate the best of all his efforts to perfect his finest poems.

—*GALWAY KINNELL*

Essential Whitman

POEMS

*Song of Myself: A Poem
of Walt Whitman, an American*

1

I celebrate myself,
And what I assume you shall assume,
For every atom belonging to me, as good belongs
    to you.

I loafe and invite my soul,
I lean and loafe at my ease, observing a spear of
    summer grass.

2

Houses and rooms are full of perfumes—the
    shelves are crowded with perfumes,
I breathe the fragrance myself, and know it and
    like it,

The distillation would intoxicate me also, but I shall
    not let it.

The atmosphere is not a perfume—it has no taste
    of the distillation, it is odorless,
It is for my mouth forever—I am in love with it,
I will go to the bank by the wood, and become
    undisguised and naked,
I am mad for it to be in contact with me.

The smoke of my own breath,
Echoes, ripples, and buzzed whispers, love-root,
    silk-thread, crotch and vine,
My respiration and inspiration, the beating of my
    heart, the passing of blood and air through
    my lungs,
The sniff of green leaves and dry leaves, and of the
    shore and dark-colored sea-rocks, and of hay in
    the barn,
The sound of the belched words of my voice, words
    loosed to the eddies of the wind,
A few light kisses, a few embraces, a reaching
    around of arms,
The play of shine and shade on the trees as the
    supple boughs wag,
The delight alone or in the rush of the streets, or
    along the fields and hillsides,
The feeling of health, the full-noon trill, the song of
    me rising from bed and meeting the sun.

Have you reckoned a thousand acres much? Have
    you reckoned the earth much?
Have you practiced so long to learn to read?
Have you felt so proud to get at the meaning of
    poems?

Stop this day and night with me and you shall
    possess the origin of all poems,
You shall possess the good of the earth and sun —
    there are millions of suns left,
You shall no longer take things at second or third
    hand, nor look through the eyes of the dead, nor
    feed on the spectres in books,
You shall not look through my eyes either, nor take
    things from me,
You shall listen to all sides and filter them from
    yourself.

3
I have heard what the talkers were talking, the talk
    of the beginning and the end,
But I do not talk of the beginning or the end.

There was never any more inception than there
    is now,
Nor any more youth or age than there is now,
And will never be any more perfection than there
    is now,
Nor any more heaven or hell than there is now.

Urge and urge and urge,
Always the procreant urge of the world.

Out of the dimness opposite equals advance—
   always substance and increase, always sex,
Always a knit of identity—always
   distinction—always a breed of life.

To elaborate is no avail—learned and unlearned
   feel that it is so.

Sure as the most certain sure, plumb in the
   uprights, well entretied, braced in the
   beams,
Stout as a horse, affectionate, haughty, electrical,
I and this mystery here we stand.

Clear and sweet is my soul, and clear and sweet is all
   that is not my soul.

Lack one lacks both, and the unseen is proved by
   the seen,
Till that becomes unseen and receives proof in
   its turn.

Showing the best and dividing it from the worst, age
   vexes age,
Knowing the perfect fitness and equanimity of
   things, while they discuss I am silent, and go
   bathe and admire myself.

Welcome is every organ and attribute of me, and
of any man hearty and clean,
Not an inch nor a particle of an inch is vile,
and none shall be less familiar than
the rest.

I am satisfied—I see, dance, laugh, sing,
As God comes a loving bed-fellow and sleeps
at my side all night and close on the peep of
the day,
And leaves for me baskets covered with white towels
bulging the house with their plenty,
Shall I postpone my acceptation and realization
and scream at my eyes,
That they turn from gazing after and down the
road,
And forthwith cipher and show me to a cent,
Exactly the contents of one, and exactly the
contents of two, and which is ahead?

4
Trippers and askers surround me,
People I meet—the effect upon me of my early life,
of the ward and city I live in, of the nation,
The latest news, discoveries, inventions, societies,
authors old and new,
My dinner, dress, associates, looks, business,
compliments, dues,
The real or fancied indifference of some man or
woman I love,

The sickness of one of my folks, or of myself, or
    ill-doing, or loss or lack of money, or depressions
    or exaltations,
They come to me days and nights and go from
    me again,
But they are not the Me myself.

Apart from the pulling and hauling stands what
    I am,
Stands amused, complacent, compassionating,
    idle, unitary,
Looks down, is erect, bends an arm on an
    impalpable certain rest,
Looks with its side-curved head curious what will
    come next,
Both in and out of the game, and watching and
    wondering at it.

Backward I see in my own days where I sweated
    through fog with linguists and contenders,
I have no mockings or arguments—I witness and
    wait.

5
I believe in you my soul—the other I am must not
    abase itself to you,
And you must not be abased to the other.

Loafe with me on the grass—loose the stop from
    your throat,

Not words, not music or rhyme I want—not custom
    or lecture, not even the best,
Only the lull I like, the hum of your valved voice.

I mind how once we lay such a transparent summer
    morning,
How you settled your head athwart my hips and
    gently turned over upon me,
And parted the shirt from my bosom-bone, and
    plunged your tongue to my bare-stript heart,
And reached till you felt my beard, and reached till
    you held my feet.

Swiftly arose and spread around me the peace
    and knowledge that pass all the argument of
    the earth,
And I know that the hand of God is the elderhand
    of my own,
And I know that the spirit of God is the brother of
    my own,
And that all the men ever born are also my brothers,
    and the women my sisters and lovers,
And that a kelson of the creation is love,
And limitless are leaves stiff or drooping in the
    fields,
And brown ants in the little wells beneath them,
And mossy scabs of the worm fence, and heaped
    stones, and elder and mullen and poke-weed.

6

A child said, What is the grass? fetching it to me
    with full hands,
How could I answer the child? I do not know what it
    is any more than he.

I guess it must be the flag of my disposition, out of
    hopeful green stuff woven.

Or I guess it is the handkerchief of the Lord,
A scented gift and remembrancer designedly
    dropped,
Bearing the owner's name someway in the corners,
    that we may see and remark, and say Whose?

Or I guess the grass is itself a child, the produced
    babe of the vegetation.

Or I guess it is a uniform hieroglyphic,
And it means, Sprouting alike in broad zones and
    narrow zones,
Growing among black folks as among white,
Kanuck, Tuckahoe, Congressman, Cuff, I give them
    the same, I receive them the same.

And now it seems to me the beautiful uncut hair of
    graves.

Tenderly will I use you curling grass,
It may be you transpire from the breasts of
    young men,

It may be if I had known them I would have loved
    them,
It may be you are from old people and from women,
    and from offspring taken soon out of their
    mothers' laps,
And here you are the mothers' laps.

This grass is very dark to be from the white heads of
    old mothers,
Darker than the colorless beards of old men,
Dark to come from under the faint red roofs of
    mouths.

O I perceive after all so many uttering tongues!
And I perceive they do not come from the roofs of
    mouths for nothing.

I wish I could translate the hints about the dead
    young men and women
And the hints about old men and mothers, and the
    offspring taken soon out of their laps.

What do you think has become of the young and
    old men?
And what do you think has become of the women
    and children?

They are alive and well somewhere,
The smallest sprout shows there is really no death,

And if ever there was it led forward life, and does
    not wait at the end to arrest it,
And ceased the moment life appeared.

All goes onward and outward—and nothing
    collapses,
And to die is different from what any one supposed,
    and luckier.

7

Has any one supposed it lucky to be born?
I hasten to inform him or her it is just as lucky to
    die, and I know it.

I pass death with the dying, and birth with the new-
    washed babe, and am not contained between my
    hat and boots,
And peruse manifold objects, no two alike, and
    every one good,
The earth good, and the stars good, and their
    adjuncts all good.

I am not an earth nor an adjunct of an earth,
I am the mate and companion of people, all just as
    immortal and fathomless as myself,
They do not know how immortal, but I know.

Every kind for itself and its own—for me mine male
    and female,

For me all that have been boys and that love women,

For me the man that is proud and feels how it stings to be slighted,

For me the sweetheart and the old maid—for me mothers and the mothers of mothers,

For me lips that have smiled, eyes that have shed tears,

For me children and the begetters of children.

Undrape! you are not guilty to me, nor stale nor discarded,

I see through the broadcloth and gingham whether or no,

And am around, tenacious, acquisitive, tireless, and can never be shaken away.

8

The little one sleeps in its cradle,

I lift the gauze and look a long time, and silently brush away flies with my hand.

The youngster and the red-faced girl turn aside up the bushy hill,

I peeringly view them from the top.

The suicide sprawls on the bloody floor of the bedroom,

It is so—I witnessed the corpse—there the pistol had fallen.

The blab of the pave, the tires of carts and sluff of
    boot-soles and talk of the promenaders,
The heavy omnibus, the driver with his
    interrogating thumb, the clank of the shod
    horses on the granite floor,
The snow-sleighs, the clinking and shouted jokes
    and pelts of snow-balls,
The hurrahs for popular favorites, the fury of
    roused mobs,
The flap of the curtained litter—the sick man
    inside, borne to the hospital,
The meeting of enemies, the sudden oath, the blows
    and fall,
The excited crowd—the policeman with his star
    quickly working his passage to the centre of the
    crowd,
The impassive stones that receive and return so
    many echoes,
The souls moving along—are they invisible while
    the least atom of the stones is visible?

What groans of over-fed or half-starved who fall on
    the flags sunstruck or in fits,
What exclamations of women taken suddenly, who
    hurry home and give birth to babes,
What living and buried speech is always vibrating
    here—what howls restrained by decorum,
Arrests of criminals, slights, adulterous offers
    made, acceptances, rejections with convex
    lips,

I mind them or the resonance of them—I come
   again and again.

9
The big doors of the country-barn stand open and
      ready,
The dried grass of the harvest-time loads the
      slow-drawn wagon,
The clear light plays on the brown gray and green
      intertinged,
The armfuls are packed to the sagging mow,
I am there—I help—I came stretched atop of the
      load,
I felt its soft jolts—one leg reclined on the other,
I jump from the cross-beams, and seize the clover
      and timothy,
And roll head over heels, and tangle my hair full
      of wisps.

10
Alone far in the wilds and mountains I hunt,
Wandering amazed at my own lightness and glee,
In the late afternoon choosing a safe spot to pass
      the night,
Kindling a fire and broiling the fresh-killed game,
Soundly falling asleep on the gathered leaves, my
      dog and gun by my side.

The Yankee clipper is under her three sky-sails—
      she cuts the sparkle and scud,

My eyes settle the land—I bend at her prow or
    shout joyously from the deck.

The boatmen and clam-diggers arose early and
    stopped for me,
I tucked my trowser-ends in my boots and went and
    had a good time,
You should have been with us that day round the
    chowder-kettle.

I saw the marriage of the trapper in the open air in
    the far-west—the bride was a red girl,
Her father and his friends sat near by cross-legged
    and dumbly smoking—they had moccasins to
    their feet and large thick blankets hanging from
    their shoulders,
On a bank lounged the trapper—he was dressed
    mostly in skins—his luxuriant beard and curls
    protected his neck,
One hand rested on his rifle—the other hand held
    firmly the wrist of the red girl,
She had long eyelashes—her head was bare—her
    coarse straight locks descended upon her
    voluptuous limbs and reached to her feet.

The runaway slave came to my house and stopped
    outside,
I heard his motions crackling the twigs of the
    woodpile,

Through the swung half-door of the kitchen I saw
    him limpsey and weak,
And went where he sat on a log, and led him in and
    assured him,
And brought water and filled a tub for his sweated
    body and bruised feet,
And gave him a room that entered from my own,
    and gave him some coarse clean clothes,
And remember perfectly well his revolving eyes and
    his awkwardness,
And remember putting plasters on the galls of his
    neck and ankles,
He staid with me a week before he was recuperated
    and passed north,
I had him sit next me at table—my firelock leaned
    in the corner.

11

Twenty-eight young men bathe by the shore,
Twenty-eight young men, and all so friendly,
Twenty-eight years of womanly life, and all so
    lonesome.

She owns the fine house by the rise of the bank,
She hides handsome and richly drest aft the blinds
    of the window.

Which of the young men does she like the best?
Ah the homeliest of them is beautiful to her.

Where are you off to, lady? for I see you,
You splash in the water there, yet stay stock still in
    your room.

Dancing and laughing along the beach came the
    twenty-ninth bather,
The rest did not see her, but she saw them and
    loved them.

The beards of the young men glistened with wet, it
    ran from their long hair,
Little streams passed all over their bodies.

An unseen hand also passed over their bodies,
It descended tremblingly from their temples
    and ribs.

The young men float on their backs, their white
    bellies swell to the sun—they do not ask who
    seizes fast to them,
They do not know who puffs and declines with
    pendant and bending arch,
They do not think whom they souse with spray.

12

The butcher-boy puts off his killing-clothes, or
    sharpens his knife at the stall in the market,
I loiter enjoying his repartee and his shuffle and
    breakdown.

Blacksmiths with grimed and hairy chests environ
    the anvil,
Each has his main-sledge—they are all out—there
    is a great heat in the fire.

From the cinder-strewed threshold I follow their
    movements,
The lithe sheer of their waists plays even with their
    massive arms,
Overhand the hammers roll—overhand so slow—
    overhand so sure,
They do not hasten, each man hits in his place.

13

The negro holds firmly the reins of his four
    horses—the block swags underneath on its
    tied-over chain,
The negro that drives the huge dray of the
    stone-yard—steady and tall he stands poised
    on one leg on the string-piece,
His blue shirt exposes his ample neck and breast
    and loosens over his hip-band,
His glance is calm and commanding—he tosses the
    slouch of his hat away from his forehead,
The sun falls on his crispy hair and moustache—
    falls on the black of his polished and perfect limbs.

I behold the picturesque giant and love him—and I
    do not stop there,
I go with the team also.

In me the caresser of life wherever moving—
    backward as well as forward slueing,
To niches aside and junior bending.

Oxen that rattle the yoke or halt in the shade, what
    is that you express in your eyes?
It seems to me more than all the print I have read in
    my life.

My tread scares the wood-drake and wood-duck on
    my distant and daylong ramble,
They rise together, they slowly circle around.
I believe in those winged purposes,
And acknowledge the red yellow and white playing
    within me,
And consider the green and violet and the tufted
    crown intentional,
And do not call the tortoise unworthy because she is
    not something else,
And the mockingbird in the swamp never studied
    the gamut, yet trills pretty well to me,
And the look of the bay mare shames silliness out
    of me.

14
The wild gander leads his flock through the cool
    night,
Ya-honk! he says, and sounds it down to me like an
    invitation,

The pert may suppose it meaningless, but I listen
    closer,
I find its purpose and place up there toward the
    November sky.

The sharp-hoofed moose of the north, the cat on
    the house-sill, the chickadee, the prairie-dog,
The litter of the grunting sow as they tug at her
    teats,
The brood of the turkey-hen, and she with her half-
    spread wings,
I see in them and myself the same old law.

The press of my foot to the earth springs a hundred
    affections,
They scorn the best I can do to relate them.

I am enamoured of growing outdoors,
Of men that live among cattle or taste of the ocean
    or woods,
Of the builders and steerers of ships, of the wielders
    of axes and mauls, of the drivers of horses,
I can eat and sleep with them week in and week out.

What is commonest and cheapest and nearest and
    easiest is Me,
Me going in for my chances, spending for vast
    returns,
Adorning myself to bestow myself on the first that
    will take me,

Not asking the sky to come down to my good will,
Scattering it freely forever.

15

The pure contralto sings in the organ loft,
The carpenter dresses his plank—the tongue of his
    foreplane whistles its wild ascending lisp,
The married and unmarried children ride home to
    their thanksgiving dinner,
The pilot seizes the king-pin, he heaves down with a
    strong arm,
The mate stands braced in the whale-boat, lance
    and harpoon are ready,
The duck-shooter walks by silent and cautious
    stretches,
The deacons are ordained with crossed hands at the
    altar,
The spinning-girl retreats and advances to the hum
    of the big wheel,
The farmer stops by the bars of a Sunday and looks
    at the oats and rye,
The lunatic is carried at last to the asylum a
    confirmed case,
He will never sleep any more as he did in the cot in
    his mother's bedroom,
The jour printer with gray head and gaunt jaws
    works at his case,
He turns his quid of tobacco, his eyes get blurred
    with the manuscript,

The malformed limbs are tied to the anatomist's
    table,
What is removed drops horribly in a pail,
The quadroon girl is sold at the stand—the
    drunkard nods by the bar-room stove,
The machinist rolls up his sleeves—the policeman
    travels his beat—the gate-keeper marks who pass,
The young fellow drives the express-wagon—I love
    him though I do not know him,
The half-breed straps on his light boots to compete
    in the race,
The western turkey-shooting draws old and young—
    some lean on their rifles, some sit on logs,
Out from the crowd steps the marksman and takes
    his position and levels his piece,
The groups of newly-come immigrants cover the
    wharf or levee,
The woolly-pates hoe in the sugar-field, the overseer
    views them from his saddle,
The bugle calls in the ball-room, the gentlemen run
    for their partners, the dancers bow to each other,
The youth lies awake in the cedar-roofed garret and
    harks to the musical rain,
The Wolverine sets traps on the creek that helps fill
    the Huron,
The reformer ascends the platform, he spouts with
    his mouth and nose,
The squaw wrapt in her yellow-hemmed cloth is
    offering moccasins and bead-bags for sale,

The connoisseur peers along the exhibition-gallery
with half-shut eyes bent sideways,

The deck-hands make fast the steamboat, the plank
is thrown for the shore-going passengers,

The young sister holds out the skein, the elder sister
winds it off in a ball and stops now and then for
the knots,

The one-year wife is recovering and happy, a week
ago she bore her first child,

The clean-haired Yankee girl works with her sewing-
machine or in the factory or mill,

The nine months' gone is in the parturition
chamber, her faintness and pains are advancing,

The paving-man leans on his two-handed
rammer—the reporter's lead flies swiftly over the
note-book—the sign-painter is lettering with red
and gold,

The canal boy trots on the tow-path—the book-
keeper counts at his desk—the shoemaker waxes
his thread,

The conductor beats time for the band and all the
performers follow him,

The child is baptised—the convert is making the
first professions,

The regatta is spread on the bay—how the white
sails sparkle!

The drover watches his drove, he sings out to them
that would stray,

The pedlar sweats with his pack on his back—the
purchaser higgles about the odd cent,

The camera and plate are prepared, the lady must
    sit for her daguerreotype,
The bride unrumples her white dress, the minute-
    hand of the clock moves slowly,
The opium eater reclines with rigid head and
    just-opened lips,
The prostitute draggles her shawl, her bonnet bobs
    on her tipsy and pimpled neck,
The crowd laugh at her blackguard oaths, the men
    jeer and wink to each other,
(Miserable! I do not laugh at your oaths nor jeer
    you,)
The President holds a cabinet council, he is
    surrounded by the great secretaries,
On the piazza walk five friendly matrons with twined
    arms,
The crew of the fish-smack pack repeated layers of
    halibut in the hold,
The Missourian crosses the plains toting his wares
    and his cattle,
The fare-collector goes through the train—he gives
    notice by the jingling of loose change,
The floor-men are laying the floor—the tinners
    are tinning the roof—the masons are calling for
    mortar,
In single file each shouldering his hod pass onward
    the laborers,
Seasons pursuing each other the indescribable
    crowd is gathered—it is the Fourth of July—
    what salutes of cannon and small arms!

Seasons pursuing each other the plougher ploughs
    and the mower mows and the winter-grain falls in
    the ground,
Off on the lakes the pike-fisher watches and waits by
    the hole in the frozen surface,
The stumps stand thick round the clearing, the
    squatter strikes deep with his axe,
The flatboatmen make fast toward dusk near the
    cotton-wood or pecan-trees,
The coon-seekers go now through the regions of
    the Red river, or through those drained by the
    Tennessee, or through those of the Arkansas,
The torches shine in the dark that hangs on the
    Chattahoochee or Altamahaw,
Patriarchs sit at supper with sons and grandsons and
    great grandsons around them,
In walls of adobie, in canvas tents, rest hunters and
    trappers after their day's sport.

The city sleeps and the country sleeps,
The living sleep for their time, the dead sleep for
    their time,
The old husband sleeps by his wife and the young
    husband sleeps by his wife,
And these one and all tend inward to me, and I
    tend outward to them,
And such as it is to be of these more or less I am.

16

I am of old and young, of the foolish as much as the
    wise,

Regardless of others, ever regardful of others,

Maternal as well as paternal, a child as well as a man,

Stuffed with the stuff that is coarse, and stuffed with
    the stuff that is fine,

One of the great nations, the nation of many
    nations — the smallest the same and the largest
    the same,

A southerner soon as a northerner, a planter
    nonchalant and hospitable,

A Yankee bound my own way, ready for trade, my
    joints the limberest joints on earth and the
    sternest joints on earth,

A Kentuckian walking the vale of the Elkhorn in my
    deer-skin leggings,

A boatman over the lakes or bays or along coasts —
    a Hoosier, a Badger, a Buckeye,

A Louisianian or Georgian, a poke-easy from
    sandhills and pines,

At home on Canadian snow-shoes or up in the bush,
    or with fishermen off Newfoundland,

At home in the fleet of ice-boats, sailing with the
    rest and tacking,

At home on the hills of Vermont or in the woods of
    Maine or the Texan ranch,

Comrade of Californians — comrade of free
    northwesterners, loving their big proportions,

Comrade of raftsmen and coalmen—comrade of
all who shake hands and welcome to drink and
meat,
A learner with the simplest, a teacher of the
thoughtfulest,
A novice beginning experient of myriads of seasons,
Of every hue and trade and rank, of every caste and
religion,
Not merely of the New World but of Africa Europe
or Asia—a wandering savage,
A farmer, mechanic, or artist, a gentleman, sailor,
lover or quaker,
A prisoner, fancy-man, rowdy, lawyer, physician or
priest.

I resist anything better than my own diversity,
And breathe the air and leave plenty after me,
And am not stuck up, and am in my place.

The moth and the fish-eggs are in their place,
The suns I see and the suns I cannot see are in their
place,
The palpable is in its place and the impalpable is in
its place.

17
These are the thoughts of all men in all ages and
lands, they are not original with me,
If they are not yours as much as mine they are
nothing or next to nothing,

If they are not the riddle and the untying of the
    riddle they are nothing,
If they are not just as close as they are distant they
    are nothing.

This is the grass that grows wherever the land is and
    the water is,
This is the common air that bathes the globe.

This is the breath of laws and songs and
    behaviour,
This is the tasteless water of souls — this is the
    true sustenance,
It is for the illiterate, it is for the judges of the
    supreme court, it is for the federal capitol and
    the state capitols,
It is for the admirable communes of literary men
    and composers and singers and lecturers and
    engineers and savans,
It is for the endless races of working people and
    farmers and seamen.

18
This is the trill of a thousand clear cornets and
    scream of the octave flute and strike of
    triangles.

I play not a march for victors only — I play great
    marches for conquered and slain persons.

Have you heard that it was good to gain the day?
I also say it is good to fall—battles are lost in the
    same spirit in which they are won.

I sound triumphal drums for the dead, I fling
    through my embouchures the loudest and gayest
    music to them,
Vivas to those who have failed, and to those whose
    war-vessels sank in the sea, and those themselves
    who sank in the sea,
And to all generals that lost engagements, and all
    overcome heroes, and the numberless unknown
    heroes equal to the greatest heroes known.

19

This is the meal pleasantly set—this is the meat and
    drink for natural hunger,
It is for the wicked just the same as the righteous—I
    make appointments with all,
I will not have a single person slighted or left away,
The kept-woman and sponger and thief are hereby
    invited, the heavy-lipped slave is invited—the
    venerealee is invited,
There shall be no difference between them and the
    rest.

This is the press of a bashful hand—this is the float
    and odor of hair,
This is the touch of my lips to yours—this is the
    murmur of yearning,

This is the far-off depth and height reflecting my
    own face,
This is the thoughtful merge of myself and the
    outlet again.

Do you guess I have some intricate purpose?
Well I have—for the April rain has, and the mica on
    the side of a rock has.

Do you take it I would astonish?
Does the daylight astonish? or the early redstart
    twittering through the woods?
Do I astonish more than they?

This hour I tell things in confidence,
I might not tell everybody but I will tell you.

20
Who goes there! hankering, gross, mystical, nude?
How is it I extract strength from the beef I eat?

What is a man anyhow? what am I? and what
    are you?
All I mark as my own you shall offset it with
    your own,
Else it were time lost listening to me.

I do not snivel that snivel the world over,
That months are vacuums and the ground but
    wallow and filth,

That life is a suck and a sell, and nothing remains at
the end but threadbare crape and tears.

Whimpering and truckling fold with powders
for invalids—conformity goes to the fourth-
removed,
I cock my hat as I please indoors or out.

Shall I pray? shall I venerate and be ceremonious?
I have pried through the strata and analyzed to a
hair,
And counselled with doctors and calculated close
and found no sweeter fat than sticks to my own
bones.

In all people I see myself, none more and not one a
barley-corn less,
And the good or bad I say of myself I say of them.

And I know I am solid and sound,
To me the converging objects of the universe
perpetually flow,
All are written to me, and I must get what the
writing means.

And I know I am deathless,
I know this orbit of mine cannot be swept by a
carpenter's compass,
I know I shall not pass like a child's carlacue cut
with a burnt stick at night.

I know I am august,
I do not trouble my spirit to vindicate itself or be
    understood,
I see that the elementary laws never apologize,
I reckon I behave no prouder than the level I plant
    my house by after all.

I exist as I am, that is enough,
If no other in the world be aware I sit content,
And if each and all be aware I sit content.

One world is aware, and by far the largest to me,
    and that is myself,
And whether I come to my own today or in ten
    thousand or ten million years,
I can cheerfully take it now, or with equal
    cheerfulness I can wait.

My foothold is tenoned and mortised in granite,
I laugh at what you call dissolution,
And I know the amplitude of time.

21
I am the poet of the body,
And I am the poet of the soul.

The pleasures of heaven are with me, and the pains
    of hell are with me,
The first I graft and increase upon myself—the
    latter I translate into a new tongue.

I am the poet of the woman the same as the man,
And I say it is as great to be a woman as to be a man,
And I say there is nothing greater than the mother
    of men.

I chant a new chant of dilation or pride,

We have had ducking and deprecating about
    enough,
I show that size is only development.

Have you outstript the rest? are you the President?
It is a trifle—they will more than arrive there every
    one, and still pass on.

I am he that walks with the tender and growing
    night,
I call to the earth and sea half-held by the night.

Press close bare-bosomed night! Press close
    magnetic nourishing night!
Night of south winds! Night of the large few stars!
Still nodding night! Mad naked summer night!

Smile O voluptuous cool-breathed earth!
Earth of the slumbering and liquid trees!
Earth of departed sunset! Earth of the mountains
    misty-topt!
Earth of the vitreous pour of the full moon just
    tinged with blue!

Earth of shine and dark mottling the tide of the
river!
Earth of the limpid gray of clouds brighter and
clearer for my sake!
Far-swooping elbowed earth! Rich apple-blossomed
earth!
Smile, for your lover comes!

Prodigal! you have given me love! Therefore I to
you give love!
O unspeakable passionate love!
Thruster holding me tight and that I hold tight!
We hurt each other as the bridegroom and the
bride hurt each other.

22

You sea! I resign myself to you also—I guess what
you mean,
I behold from the beach your crooked inviting
fingers,
I believe you refuse to go back without feeling
of me,
We must have a turn together—I undress—hurry
me out of sight of the land,
Cushion me soft, rock me in billowy drowse,
Dash me with amorous wet—I can repay you.

Sea of stretched ground-swells!
Sea breathing broad and convulsive breaths!

Sea of the brine of life! sea of unshovelled and
   always-ready graves!
Howler and scooper of storms! capricious and
   dainty sea!
I am integral with you—I too am of one phase and
   of all phases.

Partaker of influx and efflux—extoller of hate and
   conciliation,
Extoller of amies and those that sleep in each
   others' arms.

I am he attesting sympathy;
Shall I make my list of things in the house and skip
   the house that supports them?

I am the poet of commonsense and of the
   demonstrable and of immortality,
And am not the poet of goodness only—I do not
   decline to be the poet of wickedness also.

Washes and razors for foofoos—for me freckles and
   a bristling beard.

What blurt is it about virtue and about vice?
Evil propels me, and reform of evil propels me—
   I stand indifferent,
My gait is no fault-finder's or rejecter's gait,
I moisten the roots of all that has grown.

Did you fear some scrofula out of the unflagging
    pregnancy?
Did you guess the celestial laws are yet to be worked
    over and rectified?

I step up to say that what we do is right and what we
    affirm is right—and some is only the ore of right,
Witnesses of us—one side a balance and the
    antipodal side a balance,
Soft doctrine as steady help as stable doctrine,
Thoughts and deeds of the present our rouse and
    early start.

This minute that comes to me over the past
    decillions,
There is no better than it and now.

What behaved well in the past or behaves well today
    is not such a wonder,
The wonder is always and always how there can be a
    mean man or an infidel.

23
Endless unfolding of words of ages!
And mine a word of the modern—a word en masse.

A word of the faith that never balks,
One time as good as another time—here or
    henceforward it is all the same to me.

A word of reality—materialism first and last
    imbuing.

Hurrah for positive science! Long live exact
    demonstration!
Fetch stonecrop and mix it with cedar and branches
    of lilac,
This is the lexicographer or chemist—this made a
    grammar of the old cartouches,
These mariners put the ship through dangerous
    unknown seas,
This is the geologist—and this works with the
    scalpel—and this is a mathematician.

Gentlemen I receive you, and attach and clasp
    hands with you,
The facts are useful and real—they are not my
    dwelling—I enter by them to an area of the
    dwelling.

I am less the reminder of property or qualities, and
    more the reminder of life,
And go on the square for my own sake and for
    other's sake,
And make short account of neuters and geldings,
    and favor men and women fully equipped,
And beat the gong of revolt, and stop with fugitives
    and them that plot and conspire.

24

Walt Whitman, an American, one of the roughs, a
    kosmos,
Disorderly fleshy and sensual, eating drinking and
    breeding,
No sentimentalist—no stander above men and
    women or apart from them—no more modest
    than immodest.

Unscrew the locks from the doors!
Unscrew the doors themselves from their jambs!

Whoever degrades another degrades me, and
    whatever is done or said returns at last to me,
And whatever I do or say I also return.

Through me the afflatus surging and surging—
    through me the current and index.

I speak the pass-word primeval—I give the sign of
    democracy,
By God! I will accept nothing which all cannot have
    their counterpart of on the same terms.

Through me many long dumb voices,
Voices of the interminable generations of slaves,
Voices of prostitutes and of deformed persons,
Voices of the diseased and despairing, and of thieves
    and dwarfs,
Voices of cycles of preparation and accretion,

And of the threads that connect the stars—and of
    wombs, and of the father-stuff,
And of the rights of them the others are down
    upon,
Of the trivial and flat and foolish and despised,
Of fog in the air and beetles rolling balls of dung.

Through me forbidden voices,
Voices of sexes and lusts—voices veiled, and I
    remove the veil,
Voices indecent by me clarified and transfigured.

I do not press my finger across my mouth,
I keep as delicate around the bowels as around the
    head and heart,
Copulation is no more rank to me than death is.

I believe in the flesh and the appetites,
Seeing hearing and feeling are miracles, and each
    part and tag of me is a miracle.

Divine am I inside and out, and I make holy
    whatever I touch or am touched from,
The scent of these arm-pits is aroma finer than
    prayer,
This head is more than churches or bibles or
    creeds.

If I worship one thing more than another it shall be
    the spread of my own body, or any part of it.

Translucent mould of me it shall be you,
Shaded ledges and rests, firm masculine coulter, it
   shall be you,
Whatever goes to the tilth of me it shall be you,
You my rich blood, your milky stream pale
   strippings of my life,
Breast that presses against other breasts it shall
   be you,
My brain it shall be your occult convolutions,
Root of washed sweet-flag, timorous pond-snipe,
   nest of guarded duplicate eggs, it shall be you,
Mixed tussled hay of head and beard and brawn it
   shall be you,
Trickling sap of maple, fibre of manly wheat, it shall
   be you,
Sun so generous it shall be you,
Vapors lighting and shading my face it shall
   be you,
You sweaty brooks and dews it shall be you,
Winds whose soft-tickling genitals rub against me it
   shall be you,
Broad muscular fields, branches of live oak, loving
   lounger in my winding paths, it shall be you,
Hands I have taken, face I have kissed, mortal I have
   ever touched, it shall be you.

I dote on myself—there is that lot of me, and all so
   luscious,
Each moment and whatever happens thrills me
   with joy.

I cannot tell how my ankles bend, nor whence the
    cause of my faintest wish,
Nor the cause of the friendship I emit, nor the
    cause of the friendship I take again.

To walk up my stoop is unaccountable, I pause to
    consider if it really be,
That I eat and drink is spectacle enough for the
    great authors and schools,
A morning-glory at my window satisfies me more
    than the metaphysics of books.

To behold the daybreak!
The little light fades the immense and diaphanous
    shadows,
The air tastes good to my palate.

Hefts of the moving world at innocent gambols,
    silently rising, freshly exuding,
Scooting obliquely high and low.

Something I cannot see puts upward libidinous
    prongs,
Seas of bright juice suffuse heaven.

The earth by the sky staid with—the daily close of
    their junction,
The heaved challenge from the east that moment
    over my head,

The mocking taunt, See then whether you shall be
    master!

25
Dazzling and tremendous how quick the sunrise
    would kill me,
If I could not now and always send sunrise out
    of me.

We also ascend dazzling and tremendous as the sun,
We found our own my soul in the calm and cool of
    the daybreak.

My voice goes after what my eyes cannot reach,
With the twirl of my tongue I encompass worlds and
    volumes of worlds.

Speech is the twin of my vision — it is unequal to
    measure itself.

It provokes me forever,
It says sarcastically, Walt, you understand enough —
    why don't you let it out then?

Come now I will not be tantalized — you conceive
    too much of articulation.

Do you not know how the buds beneath are folded?
Waiting in gloom protected by frost,
The dirt receding before my prophetical screams,

I underlying causes to balance them at last,
My knowledge my live parts—it keeping tally with
the meaning of things,
Happiness—which whoever hears me let him or
her set out in search of this day.

My final merit I refuse you—I refuse putting from
me the best I am.

Encompass worlds but never try to encompass me,
I crowd your noisiest talk by looking toward you.

Writing and talk do not prove me,
I carry the plenum of proof and every thing else in
my face,
With the hush of my lips I confound the topmost
skeptic.

26
I think I will do nothing for a long time but listen,
And accrue what I hear into myself—and let sounds
contribute toward me.

I hear the bravuras of birds, the bustle of growing
wheat, gossip of flames, clack of sticks cooking
my meals.

I hear the sound of the human voice—a sound
I love,

I hear all sounds as they are tuned to their uses,
    sounds of the city and sounds out of the
    city—sounds of the day and night,
Talkative young ones to those that like them—the
    recitative of fish-pedlars and fruit-pedlars—the
    loud laugh of work-people at their meals,
The angry bass of disjointed friendship—the faint
    tones of the sick,
The judge with hands tight to the desk, his shaky
    lips pronouncing a death-sentence,
The heave'e'yo of stevedores unlading ships by the
    wharves—the refrain of the anchor-lifters,
The ring of alarm-bells—the cry of fire—the
    whirr of swift-streaking engines and hose-carts
    with premonitory tinkles and colored
    lights,
The steam-whistle—the solid roll of the train of
    approaching cars,
The slow-march played at night at the head of the
    association,
They go to guard some corpse—the flag-tops are
    draped with black muslin.

I hear the violincello or man's heart complaint,
And hear the keyed cornet or else the echo of
    sunset.

I hear the chorus—it is a grand-opera, this indeed
    is music!

A tenor large and fresh as the creation fills me,
The orbic flex of his mouth is pouring and filling
    me full.

I hear the trained soprano—she convulses me like
    the climax of my love-grip,
The orchestra whirls me wider than Uranus flies,
It wrenches unnamable ardors from my breast,
It throbs me to gulps of the farthest down horror,
It sails me, I dab with bare feet, they are licked by
    the indolent waves,
I am exposed, cut by bitter and poisoned hail,
Steeped amid honeyed morphine, my windpipe
    squeezed in the fakes of death,
Let up again to feel the puzzle of puzzles,
And that we call Being.

27
To be in any form, what is that?
If nothing lay more developed the quahaug and its
    callous shell were enough.

Mine is no callous shell,
I have instant conductors all over me whether I pass
    or stop,
They seize every object and lead it harmlessly
    through me.

I merely stir, press, feel with my fingers, and am
    happy,

To touch my person to some one else's is about as
    much as I can stand.

28

Is this then a touch? quivering me to a new identity,
Flames and ether making a rush for my veins,
Treacherous tip of me reaching and crowding to
    help them,
My flesh and blood playing out lightning, to strike
    what is hardly different from myself,
On all sides prurient provokers stiffening my limbs,
Straining the udder of my heart for its withheld drip,
Behaving licentious toward me, taking no denial,
Depriving me of my best as for a purpose,
Unbuttoning my clothes and holding me by the
    bare waist,
Deluding my confusion with the calm of the
    sunlight and pasture fields,
Immodestly sliding the fellow-senses away,
They bribed to swap off with touch, and go and
    graze at the edges of me,
No consideration, no regard for my draining
    strength or my anger,
Fetching the rest of the herd around to enjoy
    them awhile,
Then all uniting to stand on a headland and
    worry me.

The sentries desert every other part of me,
They have left me helpless to a red marauder,

They all come to the headland to witness and assist
   against me.

I am given up by traitors,
I talk wildly—I have lost my wits—I and nobody
   else am the greatest traitor,
I went myself first to the headland—my own hands
   carried me there.

You villain touch! what are you doing? my breath
   is tight in its throat,
Unclench your floodgates! you are too much
   for me.

29
Blind loving wrestling touch! sheathed hooded
   sharp-toothed touch!
Did it make you ache so leaving me?

Parting tracked by arriving—perpetual payment of
   the perpetual loan,
Rich showering rain, and recompense richer
   afterward.

Sprouts take and accumulate—stand by the curb
   prolific and vital,
Landscapes projected masculine full-sized and
   golden.

30

All truths wait in all things,
They neither hasten their own delivery nor resist it,
They do not need the obstetric forceps of the
    surgeon,
The insignificant is as big to me as any,
What is less or more than a touch?

Logic and sermons never convince,
The damp of the night drives deeper into my
    soul.

Only what proves itself to every man and woman
    is so,
Only what nobody denies is so.

A minute and a drop of me settle my brain,
I believe the soggy clods shall become lovers and
    lamps,
And a compend of compends is the meat of a man
    or woman,
And a summit and flower there is the feeling they
    have for each other,
And they are to branch boundlessly out of that
    lesson until it becomes omnific,
And until every one shall delight us, and we them.

31

I believe a leaf of grass is no less than the
    journeywork of the stars,

And the pismire is equally perfect, and a grain of
    sand, and the egg of the wren,
And the tree-toad is a chef-d'œuvre for the
    highest,
And the running blackberry would adorn the
    parlors of heaven,
And the narrowest hinge in my hand puts to scorn
    all machinery,
And the cow crunching with depressed head
    surpasses any statue,
And a mouse is miracle enough to stagger sextillions
    of infidels,
And I could come every afternoon of my life to look
    at the farmer's girl boiling her iron tea-kettle and
    baking shortcake.

I find I incorporate gneiss and coal and long-
    threaded moss and fruits and grains and esculent
    roots,
And am stucco'd with quadrupeds and birds all
    over,
And have distanced what is behind me for good
    reasons,
And call any thing close again when I desire it.

In vain the speeding or shyness,
In vain the plutonic rocks send their old heat
    against my approach,
In vain the mastodon retreats beneath its own
    powdered bones,

In vain objects stand leagues off and assume
    manifold shapes,
In vain the ocean settling in hollows and the great
    monsters lying low,
In vain the buzzard houses herself with the sky,
In vain the snake slides through the creepers and
    logs,
In vain the elk takes to the inner passes of the woods,
In vain the razor-billed auk sails far north to
    Labrador,
I follow quickly, I ascend to the nest in the fissure of
    the cliff.

32

I think I could turn and live awhile with the animals,
    they are so placid and self-contained,
I stand and look at them sometimes half the day
    long.

They do not sweat and whine about their condition,
They do not lie awake in the dark and weep for
    their sins,
They do not make me sick discussing their duty
    to God,
Not one is dissatisfied—not one is demented with
    the mania of owning things,
Not one kneels to another nor to his kind that lived
    thousands of years ago,
Not one is respectable or unhappy over the whole
    earth.

So they show their relations to me and I accept
    them,
They bring me tokens of myself—they evince them
    plainly in their possession.

I do not know where they got those tokens,
I must have passed that way untold times ago and
    negligently dropt them,
Myself moving forward then and now and forever,
Gathering and showing more always and with
    velocity,
Infinite and omnigenous and the like of these
    among them,
Not too exclusive toward the reachers of my
    remembrancers,
Picking out here one that shall be my amie,
Choosing to go with him on brotherly terms.

A gigantic beauty of a stallion, fresh and responsive
    to my caresses,
Head high in the forehead and wide between the
    ears,
Limbs glossy and supple, tail dusting the ground,
Eyes well apart and full of sparkling wickedness—
    ears finely cut and flexibly moving.

His nostrils dilate, my heels embrace him, his
    well-built limbs tremble with pleasure, we speed
    around and return.

I but use you a moment and then I resign you
    stallion, and do not need your paces, and
    outgallop them,
And myself as I stand or sit pass faster than you.

33
Swift wind! Space! My soul! now I know it is true
    what I guessed at,
What I guessed when I loafed on the grass,
What I guessed while I lay alone in my bed, and
    again as I walked the beach under the paling
    stars of the morning.

My ties and ballasts leave me—I travel—I sail—
    my elbows rest in the sea-gaps,
I skirt the sierras—my palms cover continents,
I am afoot with my vision.

By the city's quadrangular houses—in log-huts—
    or camping with lumbermen,
Along the ruts of the turnpike—along the dry
    gulch and rivulet bed,
Hoeing my onion-patch, and rows of carrots and
    parsnips—crossing savannas—trailing in
    forests,
Prospecting—gold-digging—girdling the trees of a
    new purchase,
Scorched ankle-deep by the hot sand—hauling my
    boat down the shallow river,

Where the panther walks to and fro on a limb
     overhead—where the buck turns furiously at the
     hunter,
Where the rattlesnake suns his flabby length on a
     rock—where the otter is feeding on fish,
Where the alligator in his tough pimples sleeps by
     the bayou,
Where the black bear is searching for roots or
     honey—where the beaver pats the mud with his
     paddle-tail,
Over the growing sugar—over the cotton plant—
     over the rice in its low moist field,
Over the sharp-peaked farmhouse with its scalloped
     scum and slender shoots from the gutters,
Over the western persimmon—over the long-leaved
     corn and the delicate blue-flowered flax,
Over the white and brown buckwheat, a hummer
     and a buzzer there with the rest,
Over the dusky green of the rye as it ripples and
     shades in the breeze,
Scaling mountains, pulling myself cautiously up,
     holding on by low scragged limbs,
Walking the path worn in the grass and beat
     through the leaves of the brush,
Where the quail is whistling betwixt the woods and
     the wheat-lot,
Where the bat flies in the July eve—where the great
     gold-bug drops through the dark,
Where the flails keep time on the barn floor,

Where the brook puts out of the roots of the old
     tree and flows to the meadow,
Where cattle stand and shake away flies with the
     tremulous shuddering of their hides,
Where the cheese-cloth hangs in the kitchen, and
     andirons straddle the hearth-slab, and cobwebs
     fall in festoons from the rafters,
Where trip-hammers crash—where the press is
     whirling its cylinders,
Wherever the human heart beats with terrible
     throes out of its ribs,
Where the pear-shaped balloon is floating aloft,
     floating in it myself and looking composedly
     down,
Where the life-car is drawn on the slip-noose—
     where the heat hatches pale-green eggs in the
     dented sand,
Where the she-whale swims with her calves and
     never forsakes them,
Where the steam-ship trails hindways its long
     pennant of smoke,
Where the ground-shark's fin cuts like a black chip
     out of the water,
Where the half-burned brig is riding on unknown
     currents,
Where shells grow to her slimy deck, and the dead
     are corrupting below,
Where the striped and starred flag is borne at the
     head of the regiments,

Approaching Manhattan, up by the long-stretching
island,
Under Niagara, the cataract falling like a veil over
my countenance,
Upon a door-step—upon the horse-block of hard
wood outside,
Upon the race-course, or enjoying picnics or jigs or
a good game of base-ball,
At he-festivals with blackguard jibes and ironical
license and bull-dances and drinking and
laughter,
At the cider-mill, tasting the sweet of the brown
sqush, sucking the juice through a straw,
At apple-peelings, wanting kisses for all the red fruit
I find,
At musters and beach-parties and friendly bees and
huskings and house-raisings,
Where the mockingbird sounds his delicious
gurgles, and cackles and screams and weeps,
Where the hay-rick stands in the barn-yard, and the
dry-stalks are scattered, and the brood cow waits
in the hovel,
Where the bull advances to do his masculine
work, and the stud to the mare, and the cock is
treading the hen,
Where the heifers browse, and the geese nip their
food with short jerks,
Where the sun-down shadows lengthen over the
limitless and lonesome prairie,

Where the herds of buffalo make a crawling spread
  of the square miles far and near,
Where the humming-bird shimmers—where
  the neck of the long-lived swan is curving and
  winding,
Where the laughing-gull scoots by the slappy shore
  and laughs her near-human laugh,
Where bee-hives range on a gray bench in the
  garden half-hid by the high weeds,
Where the band-necked partridges roost in a ring
  on the ground with their heads out,
Where burial coaches enter the arched gates of a
  cemetery,
Where winter wolves bark amid wastes of snow and
  icicled trees,
Where the yellow-crowned heron comes to the edge
  of the marsh at night and feeds upon small crabs,
Where the splash of swimmers and divers cools the
  warm noon,
Where the katy-did works her chromatic reed on the
  walnut-tree over the well,
Through patches of citrons and cucumbers with
  silver-wired leaves,
Through the salt-lick or orange glade, or under
  conical firs,
Through the gymnasium—through the curtained
  saloon—through the office or public hall,
Pleased with the native and pleased with the
  foreign—pleased with the new and old,

Pleased with women, the homely as well as the
handsome,
Pleased with the quakeress as she puts off her
bonnet and talks melodiously,
Pleased with the primitive tunes of the choir of the
whitewashed church,
Pleased with the earnest words of the sweating
Methodist preacher, or any preacher—impressed
seriously at the camp-meeting,
Looking in at the shop-windows in Broadway the
whole forenoon—pressing the flesh of my nose
to the thick plate-glass,
Wandering the same afternoon with my face turned
up to the clouds,
My right and left arms round the sides of two
friends and I in the middle,
Coming home with the bearded and dark-cheeked
bush-boy, riding behind him at the drape of
the day,
Far from the settlements studying the print of
animals' feet, or the moccasin print,
By the cot in the hospital reaching lemonade to a
feverish patient,
By the coffined corpse when all is still, examining
with a candle,
Voyaging to every port to dicker and adventure,
Hurrying with the modern crowd, as eager and
fickle as any,
Hot toward one I hate, ready in my madness to
knife him,

Solitary at midnight in my back yard, my thoughts
    gone from me a long while,
Walking the old hills of Judea with the beautiful
    gentle god by my side,
Speeding through space—speeding through
    heaven and the stars,
Speeding amid the seven satellites and the broad
    ring and the diameter of eighty thousand miles,
Speeding with tailed meteors—throwing fire-balls
    like the rest,
Carrying the crescent child that carries its own full
    mother in its belly:
Storming enjoying planning loving cautioning,
Backing and filling, appearing and disappearing,
I tread day and night such roads.

I visit the orchards of God and look at the spheric
    product,
And look at quintillions ripened, and look at
    quintillions green.

I fly the flight of the fluid and swallowing soul,
My course runs below the soundings of plummets.

I help myself to material and immaterial,
No guard can shut me off, no law can prevent me.

I anchor my ship for a little while only,
My messengers continually cruise away or bring
    their returns to me.

I go hunting polar furs and the seal—leaping
     chasms with a pike-pointed staff—clinging to
     topples of brittle and blue.

I ascend to the foretruck, I take my place late at
     night in the crow's nest, we sail through the arctic
     sea—it is plenty light enough,
Through the clear atmosphere I stretch around on
     the wonderful beauty,
The enormous masses of ice pass me and I pass
     them—the scenery is plain in all directions,
The white-topped mountains point up in the
     distance—I fling out my fancies toward
     them,
We are about approaching some great battlefield
     in which we are soon to be engaged,
We pass the colossal outposts of the encampment—
     we pass with still feet and caution,
Or we are entering by the suburbs some vast and
     ruined city, the blocks and fallen architecture
     more than all the living cities of the globe.

I am a free companion—I bivouac by invading
     watchfires.
I turn the bridegroom out of bed and stay with the
     bride myself,
And tighten her all night to my thighs and lips.

My voice is the wife's voice, the screech by the rail of
     the stairs,

They fetch my man's body up dripping and
    drowned.

I understand the large hearts of heroes,
The courage of present times and all times,
How the skipper saw the crowded and rudderless
    wreck of the steam-ship, and death chasing it up
    and down the storm,
How he knuckled tight and gave not back one inch,
    and was faithful of days and faithful of nights,
And chalked in large letters on a board, Be of good
    cheer, We will not desert you,
How he saved the drifting company at last,
How the lank loose-gowned women looked when
    boated from the side of their prepared graves,
How the silent old-faced infants, and the lifted sick,
    and the sharp-lipped unshaved men,
All this I swallow and it tastes good—I like it well,
    and it becomes mine,
I am the man—I suffered—I was there.

The disdain and calmness of martyrs,
The mother condemned for a witch and burnt with
    dry wood, and her children gazing on,
The hounded slave that flags in the race and leans
    by the fence, blowing and covered with sweat,
The twinges that sting like needles his legs and
    neck,
The murderous buckshot and the bullets,
All these I feel or am.

I am the hounded slave, I wince at the bite of the
    dogs,
Hell and despair are upon me, crack and again
    crack the marksmen,
I clutch the rails of the fence, my gore dribs thinned
    with the ooze of my skin,
I fall on the weeds and stones,
The riders spur their unwilling horses and haul
    close,
They taunt my dizzy ears, they beat me violently over
    the head with their whip-stocks.

Agonies are one of my changes of garments,
I do not ask the wounded person how he feels—
    I myself become the wounded person,
My hurt turns livid upon me as I lean on a cane and
    observe.

I am the mashed fireman with breastbone broken—
    tumbling walls buried me in their debris,
Heat and smoke I inspired—I heard the yelling
    shouts of my comrades,
I heard the distant click of their picks and shovels,
They have cleared the beams away—they tenderly
    lift me forth.

I lie in the night air in my red shirt—the pervading
    hush is for my sake,
Painless after all I lie, exhausted but not so
    unhappy,

White and beautiful are the faces around me—
    the heads are bared of their fire-caps,
The kneeling crowd fades with the light of the
    torches.

Distant and dead resuscitate,
They show as the dial or move as the hands of me—
    and I am the clock myself.

I am an old artillerist, and tell of some fort's
    bombardment, and am there again.

Again the reveille of drummers, again the attacking
    cannon and mortars and howitzers,
Again the attacked send their cannon responsive.

I take part—I see and hear the whole,
The cries and curses and roar—the plaudits for
    well-aimed shots,
The ambulanza slowly passing and trailing its red
    drip,
Workmen searching after damages and to make
    indispensable repairs,
The fall of grenades through the rent roof—the
    fan-shaped explosion,
The whizz of limbs heads stone wood and iron high
    in the air.

Again gurgles the mouth of my dying general—
    he furiously waves with his hand,

He gasps through the clot, Mind not me—mind—
    the entrenchments.

34
I tell not the fall of Alamo, not one escaped to tell
    the fall of Alamo,
The hundred and fifty are dumb yet at Alamo.

Hear now the tale of a jetblack sunrise,
Hear of the murder in cold blood of four hundred
    and twelve young men.

Retreating they had formed in a hollow square with
    their baggage for breastworks,
Nine hundred lives out of the surrounding enemy's
    nine times their number was the price they took
    in advance,
Their colonel was wounded and their ammunition
    gone,
They treated for an honorable capitulation,
    received writing and seal, gave up their arms, and
    marched back prisoners of war.

They were the glory of the race of rangers,
Matchless with a horse, a rifle, a song, a supper or a
    courtship,
Large, turbulent, brave, handsome, generous,
    proud and affectionate,

Bearded, sunburnt, dressed in the free costume of
    hunters,
Not a single one over thirty years of age.

The second Sunday morning they were brought out
    in squads and massacred—it was beautiful early
    summer,
The work commenced about five o'clock and was
    over by eight.

None obeyed the command to kneel,
Some made a mad and helpless rush—some stood
    stark and straight,
A few fell at once, shot in the temple or heart—the
    living and dead lay together,
The maimed and mangled dug in the dirt—the
    new-comers saw them there,
Some half-killed attempted to crawl away,
These were dispatched with bayonets or battered
    with the blunts of muskets,
A youth not seventeen years old seized his assassin
    till two more came to release him,
The three were all torn, and covered with the boy's
    blood.

At eleven o'clock began the burning of the bodies,
And that is the tale of the murder of the four
    hundred and twelve young men,
And that was a jetblack sunrise.

35

Did you read in the seabooks of the old-fashioned
    frigate-fight?
Did you learn who won by the light of the moon
    and stars?

Our foe was no skulk in his ship, I tell you,
His was the English pluck, and there is no
    tougher or truer, and never was, and never
    will be,
Along the lowered eve he came, horribly
    raking us.

We closed with him—the yards entangled—
    the cannon touched,
My captain lashed fast with his own hands.

We had received some eighteen-pound shots under
    the water,
On our lower-gun-deck two large pieces had burst
    at the first fire, killing all around and blowing up
    overhead.

Ten o'clock at night, and the full moon shining
    and the leaks on the gain, and five feet of water
    reported,
The master-at-arms loosing the prisoners confined
    in the after-hold to give them a chance for
    themselves.

The transit to and from the magazine was now
    stopped by the sentinels,
They saw so many strange faces they did not know
    whom to trust.

Our frigate was afire, the other asked if we
    demanded quarter? if our colors were struck and
    the fighting done?

I laughed content when I heard the voice of my
    little captain,
We have not struck, he composedly cried, We have
    just begun our part of the fighting.

Only three guns were in use,
One was directed by the captain himself against the
    enemy's main-mast,
Two well-served with grape and canister silenced his
    musketry and cleared his decks.

The tops alone seconded the fire of this little
    battery, especially the maintop,
They all held out bravely during the whole of the
    action.

Not a moment's cease,
The leaks gained fast on the pumps—the fire eats
    toward the powder-magazine,
One of the pumps was shot away—it was generally
    thought we were sinking.

Serene stood the little captain,

He was not hurried—his voice was neither high
nor low,

His eyes gave more light to us than our battle-
lanterns.

Toward twelve at night, there in the beams of the
moon they surrendered to us.

36
Stretched and still lay the midnight,

Two great hulls motionless on the breast of the
darkness,

Our vessel riddled and slowly sinking—preparations
to pass to the one we had conquered,

The captain on the quarter-deck coldly giving his
orders through a countenance white as a sheet,

Near by the corpse of the child that served in the
cabin,

The dead face of an old salt with long white hair
and carefully curled whiskers,

The flames spite of all that could be done flickering
aloft and below,

The husky voices of the two or three officers yet fit
for duty,

Formless stacks of bodies and bodies by
themselves—dabs of flesh upon the masts
and spars,

The cut of cordage and dangle of rigging, the slight
shock of the soothe of waves,

Black and impassive guns, and litter of powder-
    parcels, and the strong scent,
Delicate sniffs of the sea-breeze, smells of sedgy
    grass and fields by the shore, death-messages
    given in charge to survivors,
The hiss of the surgeon's knife and the gnawing
    teeth of his saw,
The wheeze, the cluck, the swash of falling blood,
    the short wild scream, the long dull tapering
    groan,
These so—these irretrievable.

37
O Christ! My fit is mastering me!
Through the conquered doors they crowd. I am
    possessed.

I become any presence or truth of humanity here,
And see myself in prison shaped like another man,
And feel the dull unintermitted pain.

For me the keepers of convicts shoulder their
    carbines and keep watch,
It is I let out in the morning and barred at night.

Not a mutineer walks handcuffed to the jail, but I
    am handcuffed to him and walk by his side,
I am less the jolly one there, and more the silent
    one with sweat on my twitching lips.

Not a youngster is taken for larceny, but I go too
    and am tried and sentenced.

Not a cholera patient lies at the last gasp, but I also
    lie at the last gasp,
My face is ash-colored, my sinews gnarl—away from
    me people retreat.

Askers embody themselves in me, and I am
    embodied in them,
I project my hat and sit shamefaced and beg.

38
Somehow I have been stunned. Stand back!
Give me a little time beyond my cuffed head and
    slumbers and dreams and gaping,
I discover myself on a verge of the usual mistake.

That I could forget the mockers and insults!
That I could forget the trickling tears and the blows
    of the bludgeons and hammers!
That I could look with a separate look on my own
    crucifixion and bloody crowning!

I remember, I resume the overstaid fraction,
The grave of rock multiplies what has been confided
    to it, or to any graves,
The corpses rise, the gashes heal, the fastenings
    roll away.

I troop forth replenished with supreme power, one
    of an average unending procession,
We walk the roads of Ohio and Massachusetts
    and Virginia and Wisconsin and New York and
    New Orleans and Texas and Montreal and San
    Francisco and Charleston and Savannah and
    Mexico,
Inland and by the sea-coast and boundary lines, and
    we pass the boundary lines.

Our swift ordinances are on their way over the
    whole earth,
The blossoms we wear in our hats are the growth of
    two thousand years.

Eleves I salute you,
I see the approach of your numberless gangs—I see
    you understand yourselves and me,
And know that they who have eyes are divine, and
    the blind and lame are equally divine,
And that my steps drag behind yours yet go before
    them,
And are aware how I am with you no more than I
    am with everybody.

39
The friendly and flowing savage, who is he?
Is he waiting for civilization or past it and
    mastering it?

Is he some southwesterner raised outdoors? is he
    Canadian?
Is he from the Mississippi country? or from Iowa,
    Oregon or California? or from the mountains? or
    prairie life or bush-life? or from the sea?

Wherever he goes men and women accept and
    desire him,
They desire he should like them and touch them
    and speak to them and stay with them.

Behaviour lawless as snow-flakes, words simple
    as grass, uncombed head and laughter and
    naivete,
Slow-stepping feet and the common features, and
    the common modes and emanations,
They descend in new forms from the tips of his
    fingers,
They are wafted with the odor of his body or
    breath—they fly out of the glance of his eyes.

40
Flaunt of the sunshine I need not your bask—lie
    over,
You light surfaces only—I force the surfaces and
    the depths also.

Earth! you seem to look for something at my hands,
Say old topknot! what do you want?

Man or woman! I might tell how I like you, but
    cannot,
And might tell what it is in me and what it is in you,
    but cannot,
And might tell the pinings I have — the pulse of my
    nights and days.

Behold I do not give lectures or a little charity,
What I give I give out of myself.

You there, impotent, loose in the knees, open your
    scarfed chops till I blow grit within you,
Spread your palms and lift the flaps of your pockets,
I am not to be denied — I compel — I have stores
    plenty and to spare,
And any thing I have I bestow.

I do not ask who you are — that is not important
    to me,
You can do nothing and be nothing but what I will
    infold you.

To a drudge of the cotton-fields or emptier of
    privies I lean — on his right cheek I put the
    family kiss,
And in my soul I swear I never will deny him.

On women fit for conception I start bigger and
    nimbler babes,

This day I am jetting the stuff of far more arrogant
    republics.

To any one dying—thither I speed and twist the
    knob of the door,
Turn the bed-clothes toward the foot of the bed,
Let the physician and the priest go home.

I seize the descending man, I raise him with
    resistless will.

O despairer, here is my neck,
By God! you shall not go down! hang your whole
    weight upon me.

I dilate you with tremendous breath—I buoy
    you up,
Every room of the house do I fill with an armed
    force, lovers of me, bafflers of graves.

Sleep! I and they keep guard all night,
Not doubt, not decease shall dare to lay finger
    upon you,
I have embraced you, and henceforth possess you
    to myself,
And when you rise in the morning you will find
    what I tell you is so.

41

I am he bringing help for the sick as they pant on
their backs,
And for strong upright men I bring yet more
needed help.

I heard what was said of the universe,
Heard it and heard it of several thousand
years,
It is middling well as far as it goes—but is
that all?

Magnifying and applying come I,
Outbidding at the start the old cautious hucksters,
The most they offer for mankind and eternity less
than a spirt of my own seminal wet,
Taking myself the exact dimensions of Jehovah and
laying them away,
Lithographing Kronos and Zeus his son, and
Hercules his grandson,
Buying drafts of Osiris and Isis and Belus and
Brahma and Adonai,
In my portfolio placing Manito loose, and Allah on
a leaf, and the crucifix engraved,
With Odin, and the hideous-faced Mexitli, and all
idols and images,
Honestly taking them all for what they are worth,
and not a cent more,
Admitting they were alive and did the work of
their day,

Admitting they bore mites as for unfledged birds
who have now to rise and fly and sing for
themselves,
Accepting the rough deific sketches to fill out better
in myself—bestowing them freely on each man
and woman I see,
Discovering as much or more in a framer framing a
house,
Putting higher claims for him there with his
rolled-up sleeves, driving the mallet and
chisel,
Not objecting to special revelations—considering a
curl of smoke or a hair on the back of my hand as
curious as any revelation,
Those ahold of fire-engines and hook-and-ladder
ropes more to me than the gods of the antique
wars,
Minding their voices' peal through the crash of
destruction,
Their brawny limbs passing safe over charred
laths—their white foreheads whole and unhurt
out of the flames,
By the mechanic's wife with her babe at her nipple
interceding for every person born,
Three scythes at harvest whizzing in a row from
three lusty angels with shirts bagged out at their
waists,
The snag-toothed hostler with red hair redeeming
sins past and to come,

Selling all he possesses and traveling on foot to fee
  lawyers for his brother and sit by him while he is
  tried for forgery,
What was strewn in the amplest strewing the square
  rod about me, and not filling the square rod
  then,
The bull and the bug never worshipped half
  enough,
Dung and dirt more admirable than was
  dreamed,
The supernatural of no account—myself
  waiting my time to be one of the supremes,
The day getting ready for me when I shall do as
  much good as the best, and be as prodigious,
Guessing when I am it will not tickle me much to
  receive puffs out of pulpit or print,
By my life-lumps! becoming already a creator!
Putting myself here and now to the ambushed
  womb of the shadows!

42

A call in the midst of the crowd,
My own voice, orotund sweeping and final.

Come my children,
Come my boys and girls, and my women and
  household and intimates,
Now the performer launches his nerve—he has
  passed his prelude on the reeds within.

Easily written loose-fingered chords! I feel the
    thrum of their climax and close.

My head slues round on my neck,
Music rolls, but not from the organ, folks are
    around me, but they are no household of mine.

Ever the hard and unsunk ground,
Ever the eaters and drinkers—ever the upward and
    downward sun—ever the air and the ceaseless
    tides,
Ever myself and my neighbors, refreshing and
    wicked and real,
Ever the old inexplicable query—ever that thorned
    thumb—that breath of itches and thirsts,
Ever the vexer's hoot! hoot! till we find where the
    sly one hides and bring him forth,
Ever love—ever the sobbing liquid of life,
Ever the bandage under the chin—ever the trestles
    of death.

Here and there with dimes on the eyes walking,
To feed the greed of the belly the brains liberally
    spooning,
Tickets buying or taking or selling, but in to the
    feast never once going,
Many sweating and ploughing and thrashing, and
    then the chaff for payment receiving,
A few idly owning, and they the wheat continually
    claiming.

This is the city—and I am one of the citizens,
Whatever interests the rest interests me—politics,
    churches, newspapers, schools,
Benevolent societies, improvements, banks, tariffs,
    steam-ships, factories, markets,
Stocks and stores and real estate and personal
    estate.

They who piddle and patter here in collars and
    tailed coats—I am aware who they are—and
    that they are not worms or fleas,
I acknowledge the duplicates of myself under
    all the scrape-lipped and pipe-legged
    concealments.

The weakest and shallowest is deathless with me,
What I do and say the same waits for them,
Every thought that flounders in me the same
    flounders in them.

I know perfectly well my own egotism,
And know my omnivorous words, and cannot say
    any less,
And would fetch you whoever you are flush with
    myself.

My words are words of a questioning, and to
    indicate reality;
This printed and bound book—but the printer and
    the printing-office boy?

The marriage estate and settlement—but the body
and mind of the bridegroom? also those of the
bride?

The panorama of the sea—but the sea itself?

The well-taken photographs—but your wife or
friend close and solid in your arms?

The fleet of ships of the line and all the modern
improvements—but the craft and pluck of the
admiral?

The dishes and fare and furniture—but the host
and hostess, and the look out of their eyes?

The sky up there—yet here or next door or across
the way?

The saints and sages in history—but you yourself?

Sermons and creeds and theology—but the human
brain, and what is called reason, and what is
called love, and what is called life?

43

I do not despise you priests,

My faith is the greatest of faiths and the least of
faiths,

Enclosing all worship ancient and modern, and all
between ancient and modern,

Believing I shall come again upon the earth after
five thousand years,

Waiting responses from oracles, honoring the gods,
saluting the sun,

Making a fetish of the first rock or stump, powowing
with sticks in the circle of obis,

Helping the lama or brahmin as he trims the lamps
of the idols,
Dancing yet through the streets in a phallic
procession—rapt and austere in the woods, a
gymnosophist,
Drinking mead from the skull-cup—to shasta and
vedas admirant—minding the koran,
Walking the teokallis, spotted with gore from the
stone and knife—beating the serpent-skin
drum,
Accepting the gospels, accepting him that was
crucified, knowing assuredly that he is divine,
To the mass kneeling, to the puritan's prayer rising,
sitting patiently in a pew,
Ranting and frothing in my insane crisis, waiting
dead-like till my spirit arouses me,
Looking forth on pavement and land, and outside
of pavement and land,
Belonging to the winders of the circuit of circuits.

One of that centripetal and centrifugal gang,
I turn and talk like a man leaving charges before a
journey.

Down-hearted doubters, dull and excluded,
Frivolous sullen moping angry affected
disheartened atheistical,
I know every one of you, and know the unspoken
interrogatories,
By experience I know them.

How the flukes splash!
How they contort rapid as lightning, with spasms
    and spouts of blood!

Be at peace bloody flukes of doubters and sullen
    mopers,
I take my place among you as much as among any,
The past is the push of you and me and all precisely
    the same,
And the day and night are for you and me and all,
And what is yet untried and afterward is for you and
    me and all.

I do not know what is untried and afterward,
But I know it is sure and alive and sufficient.

Each who passes is considered, and each who
    stops is considered, and not a single one can
    it fail.

It cannot fail the young man who died and was
    buried,
Nor the young woman who died and was put by his
    side,
Nor the little child that peeped in at the door and
    then drew back and was never seen again,
Nor the old man who has lived without purpose,
    and feels it with bitterness worse than gall,
Nor him in the poor house tubercled by rum and
    the bad disorder,

Nor the numberless slaughtered and wrecked—nor
the brutish koboo, called the ordure of humanity,
Nor the sacs merely floating with open mouths for
food to slip in,
Nor any thing in the earth, or down in the oldest
graves of the earth,
Nor any thing in the myriads of spheres, nor one of
the myriads of myriads that inhabit them,
Nor the present, nor the least wisp that is known.

44
It is time to explain myself—let us stand up.

What is known I strip away—I launch all men and
women forward with me into the unknown.

The clock indicates the moment—but what does
eternity indicate?

Eternity lies in bottomless reservoirs—its buckets
are rising forever and ever,
They pour and they pour and they exhale away.

We have thus far exhausted trillions of winters and
summers,
There are trillions ahead, and trillions ahead of
them.

Births have brought us richness and variety,
And other births will bring us richness and variety.

I do not call one greater and one smaller,
That which fills its period and place is equal to any.

Were mankind murderous or jealous upon you my
  brother or my sister?
I am sorry for you—they are not murderous or
  jealous upon me,
All has been gentle with me—I keep no account
  with lamentation,
What have I to do with lamentation?

I am an acme of things accomplished, and I an
  encloser of things to be.

My feet strike an apex of the apices of the stairs,
On every step bunches of ages, and larger bunches
  between the steps,
All below duly traveled, and still I mount and
  mount.

Rise after rise bow the phantoms behind me,
Afar down I see the huge first Nothing, the vapor
  from the nostrils of death,
I know I was even there, I waited unseen and always,
And slept while God carried me through the
  lethargic mist,
And took my time, and took no hurt from the fœtid
  carbon.

Long I was hugged close—long and long.

Immense have been the preparations for me,
Faithful and friendly the arms that have helped me.

Cycles ferried my cradle, rowing and rowing like
    cheerful boatmen,
For room to me stars kept aside in their own
    rings,
They sent influences to look after what was to
    hold me.

Before I was born out of my mother generations
    guided me,
My embryo has never been torpid — nothing could
    overlay it,
For it the nebula cohered to an orb — the long slow
    strata piled to rest it on — vast vegetables gave it
    sustenance,
Monstrous sauroids transported it in their mouths
    and deposited it with care.

All forces have been steadily employed to complete
    and delight me,
Now I stand on this spot with my soul.

45
Span of youth! ever-pushed elasticity! Manhood
    balanced and florid and full.

My lovers suffocate me!
Crowding my lips, and thick in the pores of my skin,

Jostling me through streets and public halls—
 coming naked to me at night,
Crying by day Ahoy from the rocks of the river—
 swinging and chirping over my head,
Calling my name from flowerbeds or vines or
 tangled underbrush,
Or while I swim in the bath, or drink from the
 pump at the corner—or the curtain is down at
 the opera, or I glimpse at a woman's face in the
 railroad car,
Lighting on every moment of my life,
Bussing my body with soft and balsamic busses,
Noiselessly passing handfuls out of their hearts and
 giving them to be mine.

Old age superbly rising! ineffable grace of dying
 days!

Every condition promulges not only itself—it
 promulges what grows after and out of itself,
And the dark hush promulges as much as any.

I open my scuttle at night and see the far-sprinkled
 systems,
And all I see, multiplied as high as I can cipher,
 edge but the rim of the farther systems.

Wider and wider they spread, expanding and always
 expanding,
Outward and outward and forever outward.

My sun has his sun, and round him obediently
  wheels,
He joins with his partners a group of superior
  circuit,
And greater sets follow, making specks of the
  greatest inside them.

There is no stoppage, and never can be stoppage,
If I and you and the worlds and all beneath or upon
  their surfaces, and all the palpable life, were this
  moment reduced back to a pallid float, it would
  not avail in the long run,
We should surely bring up again where we now
  stand,
And as surely go as much farther, and then farther
  and farther.

A few quadrillions of eras, a few octillions of cubic
  leagues, do not hazard the span, or make it
  impatient,
They are but parts—any thing is but a part.

See ever so far, there is limitless space outside of
  that,
Count ever so much, there is limitless time around
  that.

Our rendezvous is fitly appointed, God will be there
  and wait till we come.

46

I know I have the best of time and space, and that I
was never measured, and never will be measured.

I tramp a perpetual journey,
My signs are a rain-proof coat and good shoes and a
staff cut from the woods,
No friend of mine takes his ease in my chair,
I have no chair, nor church nor philosophy,
I lead no man to a dinner-table or library or
exchange,
But each man and each woman of you I lead upon
a knoll,
My left hand hooking you round the waist,
My right hand pointing to landscapes of continents,
and the public road.

Not I, not any one else can travel that road for you,
You must travel it for yourself.

It is not far—it is within reach,
Perhaps you have been on it since you were born,
and did not know,
Perhaps it is every where on water and on land.

Shoulder your duds, and I will mine, and let us
hasten forth,
Wonderful cities and free nations we shall fetch as
we go.

If you tire, give me both burdens, and rest the chuff
of your hand on my hip,
And in due time you shall repay the same service
to me,
For after we start we never lie by again.

This day before dawn I ascended a hill and looked
at the crowded heaven,
And I said to my spirit, When we become the
enfolders of those orbs and the pleasure and
knowledge of every thing in them, shall we be
filled and satisfied then?
And my spirit said No, we but level that lift to pass
and continue beyond.

You are also asking me questions, and I hear you,
I answer that I cannot answer—you must find out
for yourself.

Sit awhile wayfarer,
Here are biscuits to eat and here is milk to drink,
But as soon as you sleep and renew yourself in sweet
clothes I kiss you with a goodbye kiss and open
the gate for your egress hence.

Long enough have you dreamed contemptible
dreams,
Now I wash the gum from your eyes,
You must habit yourself to the dazzle of the light
and of every moment of your life.

Long have you timidly waded, holding a plank by
    the shore,
Now I will you to be a bold swimmer,
To jump off in the midst of the sea, and rise again
    and nod to me and shout, and laughingly dash
    with your hair.

47
I am the teacher of athletes,
He that by me spreads a wider breast than my own
    proves the width of my own,
He most honors my style who learns under it to
    destroy the teacher.

The boy I love, the same becomes a man not
    through derived power but in his own right,
Wicked, rather than virtuous out of conformity or
    fear,
Fond of his sweetheart, relishing well his steak,
Unrequited love or a slight cutting him worse than a
    wound cuts,
First rate to ride, to fight, to hit the bull's eye, to sail
    a skiff, to sing a song or play on the banjo,
Preferring scars and faces pitted with smallpox over
    all latherers and those that keep out of the sun.

I teach straying from me, yet who can stray
    from me?
I follow you whoever you are from the present hour,
My words itch at your eyes till you understand them.

I do not say these things for a dollar, or to fill up the
    time while I wait for a boat,
It is you talking just as much as myself—I act as the
    tongue of you,
It was tied in your mouth, in mine it begins to be
    loosened.

I swear I will never mention love or death inside a
    house,
And I swear I never will translate myself at all, only
    to him or her who privately stays with me in the
    open air.

If you would understand me go to the heights or
    water-shore,
The nearest gnat is an explanation and a drop or
    the motion of waves a key,
The maul the oar and the handsaw second my
    words.

No shuttered room or school can commune
    with me,
But roughs and little children better than they.

The young mechanic is closest to me—he knows
    me pretty well,
The woodman that takes his axe and jug with him
    shall take me with him all day,
The farmboy ploughing in the field feels good at
    the sound of my voice,

In vessels that sail my words must sail—I go with
    fishermen and seamen, and love them,
My face rubs to the hunter's face when he lies down
    alone in his blanket,
The driver thinking of me does not mind the jolt of
    his wagon,
The young mother and old mother shall
    comprehend me,
The girl and the wife rest the needle a moment and
    forget where they are,
They and all would resume what I have told them.

48

I have said that the soul is not more than the body,
And I have said that the body is not more than the
    soul,
And nothing, not God, is greater to one than
    one's-self is,
And whoever walks a furlong without sympathy
    walks to his own funeral, dressed in his shroud,
And I or you pocketless of a dime may purchase the
    pick of the earth,
And to glance with an eye or show a bean in its pod
    confounds the learning of all times,
And there is no trade or employment but the young
    man following it may become a hero,
And there is no object so soft but it makes a hub for
    the wheeled universe,
And any man or woman shall stand cool and
    supercilious before a million universes.

And I call to mankind, Be not curious about God,
For I who am curious about each am not curious
    about God,
No array of terms can say how much I am at peace
    about God and about death.

I hear and behold God in every object, yet I
    understand God not in the least,
Nor do I understand who there can be more
    wonderful than myself.

Why should I wish to see God better than this day?
I see something of God each hour of the twenty-
    four, and each moment then,
In the faces of men and women I see God, and in
    my own face in the glass,
I find letters from God dropped in the street, and
    every one is signed by God's name,
And I leave them where they are, for I know that
    others will punctually come forever and ever.

49
And as to you death, and you bitter hug of mortality,
    it is idle to try to alarm me.

To his work without flinching the accoucheur comes,
I see the elderhand pressing receiving supporting,
I recline by the sills of the exquisite flexible doors,
    and mark the outlet, and mark the relief and
    escape.

And as to you corpse I think you are good manure,
but that does not offend me,
I smell the white roses sweet-scented and growing,
I reach to the leafy lips—I reach to the polished
breasts of melons.

And as to you life, I reckon you are the leavings of
many deaths,
No doubt I have died myself ten thousand times
before.

I hear you whispering there O stars of heaven,
O sun! O grass of graves! O perpetual transfers and
promotions! if you do not say anything how can I
say anything?

Of the turbid pool that lies in the autumn forest,
Of the moon that descends the steeps of the
soughing twilight,
Toss, sparkles of day and dusk! toss on the black
stems that decay in the muck,
Toss to the moaning gibberish of the dry limbs.

I ascend from the moon, I ascend from the night,
And perceive of the ghastly glitter the sunbeams
reflected,
And debouch to the steady and central from the
offspring great or small.

50

There is that in me—I do not know what it is—but
　　I know it is in me.

Wrenched and sweaty—calm and cool then my
　　body becomes, I sleep—I sleep long.

I do not know it—it is without name—it is a word
　　unsaid,
It is not in any dictionary or utterance or symbol.

Something it swings on more than the earth I
　　swing on,
To it the creation is the friend whose embracing
　　awakes me.

Perhaps I might tell more. Outlines! I plead for my
　　brothers and sisters.

Do you see O my brothers and sisters?
It is not chaos or death—it is form and union and
　　plan—it is eternal life—it is happiness.

51

The past and present wilt—I have filled them and
　　emptied them,
And proceed to fill my next fold of the future.

Listener up there! what have you to confide to me?
Look in my face while I snuff the sidle of evening,

Talk honestly, for no one else hears you, and I stay
   only a minute longer.

Do I contradict myself?
Very well then, I contradict myself,
I am large—I contain multitudes.

I concentrate toward them that are nigh—I wait on
   the door-slab.

Who has done his day's work and will soonest be
   through with his supper?
Who wishes to walk with me?

Will you speak before I am gone? Will you prove
   already too late?

52
The spotted hawk swoops by and accuses me—he
   complains of my gab and my loitering.

I too am not a bit tamed—I too am untranslatable,
I sound my barbaric yawp over the roofs of the
   world.

The last scud of day holds back for me,
It flings my likeness after the rest and true as any on
   the shadowed wilds,
It coaxes me to the vapor and the dusk.

I depart as air—I shake my white locks at the
    runaway sun,
I effuse my flesh in eddies and drift it in lacy jags.

I bequeath myself to the dirt to grow from the grass
    I love,
If you want me again look for me under your
    boot-soles.

You will hardly know who I am or what I mean,
But I shall be good health to you nevertheless,
And filter and fibre your blood.

Failing to fetch me at first keep encouraged,
Missing me one place search another,
I stop some where waiting for you.

Sleep-Chasings

1
I wander all night in my vision,
Stepping with light feet, swiftly and noiselessly
    stepping and stopping,
Bending with open eyes over the shut eyes of
    sleepers,
Wandering and confused, lost to myself, ill-assorted,
    contradictory,
Pausing and gazing and bending and stopping.

How solemn they look there, stretched and still,
How quiet they breathe, the little children in their
cradles.

The wretched features of ennuyees, the white
features of corpses, the livid faces of drunkards,
the sick-gray faces of onanists,
The gashed bodies on battlefields, the insane in
their strong-doored rooms, the sacred idiots,
The newborn emerging from gates and the dying
emerging from gates,
The night pervades them and enfolds them.

The married couple sleep calmly in their bed, he
with his palm on the hip of the wife, and she with
her palm on the hip of the husband,
The sisters sleep lovingly side by side in their bed,
The men sleep lovingly side by side in theirs,
And the mother sleeps, with her little child carefully
wrapped.

The blind sleep, and the deaf and dumb sleep,
The prisoner sleeps well in the prison — the
runaway son sleeps,
The murderer that is to be hung next day — how
does he sleep?
And the murdered person — how does he sleep?

The female that loves unrequited sleeps,
And the male that loves unrequited sleeps,

The head of the money-maker that plotted all day
    sleeps,
And the enraged and treacherous dispositions—all,
    all sleep.

I stand in the dark with drooping eyes by the worst-
    suffering and restless,
I pass my hands soothingly to and fro a few inches
    from them,
The restless sink in their beds—they fitfully sleep.

The earth recedes from me into the night,
I saw that it was beautiful, and I see that what is not
    the earth is beautiful.

I go from bedside to bedside—I sleep close with the
    other sleepers, each in turn,
I dream in my dream all the dreams of the other
    dreamers,
And I become the other dreamers.

I am a dance—play up there! the fit is whirling me
    fast.

I am the everlaughing—it is new moon and
    twilight,
I see the hiding of douceurs—I see nimble ghosts
    whichever way I look,
Cache, and cache again, deep in the ground and
    sea, and where it is neither ground or sea.

Well do they do their jobs, those journeymen divine,
Only from me can they hide nothing, and would
    not if they could,
I reckon I am their boss, and they make me a pet
    besides,
And surround me and lead me, and run ahead
    when I walk,
To lift their cunning covers, to signify me with
    stretched arms, and resume the way;
Onward we move! a gay gang of blackguards! with
    mirth-shouting music and wild-flapping pennants
    of joy!

I am the actor and the actress, the voter, the
    politician,
The emigrant and the exile, the criminal that stood
    in the box,
He who has been famous, and he who shall be
    famous after to-day,
The stammerer, the well-formed person, the wasted
    or feeble person.

I am she who adorned herself and folded her hair
    expectantly,
My truant lover has come, and it is dark.

Double yourself and receive me darkness,
Receive me and my lover too—he will not let me go
    without him.

I roll myself upon you as upon a bed—I resign
  myself to the dusk.

He whom I call answers me and takes the place of
  my lover,
He rises with me silently from the bed.

Darkness you are gentler than my lover—his flesh
  was sweaty and panting,
I feel the hot moisture yet that he left me.

My hands are spread forth, I pass them in all
  directions,
I would sound up the shadowy shore to which you
  are journeying.

Be careful, darkness—already, what was it
  touched me?
I thought my lover had gone, else darkness and he
  are one,
I hear the heart-beat—I follow, I fade away.

O hot-cheeked and blushing! O foolish hectic!
O for pity's sake, no one must see me now! my
  clothes were stolen while I was abed,
Now I am thrust forth, where shall I run?

Pier that I saw dimly last night when I looked from
  the windows,

Pier out from the main, let me catch myself with you
	and stay—I will not chafe you,
I feel ashamed to go naked about the world.
I am curious to know where my feet stand—and
	what is this flooding me, childhood or
	manhood—and the hunger that crosses the
	bridge between.

The cloth laps a first sweet eating and drinking,
Laps life-swelling yolks—laps ear of rose-corn, milky
	and just ripened,
The white teeth stay, and the boss-tooth advances in
	darkness,
And liquor is spilled on lips and bosoms by touching
	glasses, and the best liquor afterward.

2
I descend my western course, my sinews are flaccid,
Perfume and youth course through me, and I am
	their wake.

It is my face yellow and wrinkled instead of the old
	woman's,
I sit low in a straw-bottom chair and carefully darn
	my grandson's stockings.

It is I too, the sleepless widow looking out on the
	winter midnight,
I see the sparkles of starshine on the icy and pallid
	earth.

A shroud I see—and I am the shroud, I wrap a body
    and lie in the coffin,
It is dark here under-ground—it is not evil or pain
    here—it is blank here, for reasons.

It seems to me that everything in the light and air
    ought to be happy,
Whoever is not in his coffin and the dark grave, let
    him know he has enough.

3
I see a beautiful gigantic swimmer swimming naked
    through the eddies of the sea,
His brown hair lies close and even to his head—he
    strikes out with courageous arms, he urges
    himself with his legs.

I see his white body—I see his undaunted eyes,
I hate the swift-running eddies that would dash him
    headforemost on the rocks.

What are you doing you ruffianly red-trickled
    waves?
Will you kill the courageous giant? Will you kill him
    in the prime of his middle age?

Steady and long he struggles,
He is baffled and banged and bruised—he holds
    out while his strength holds out,

The slapping eddies are spotted with his blood—
    they bear him away—they roll him and swing
    him and turn him,
His beautiful body is borne in the circling eddies, it
    is continually bruised on rocks,
Swiftly and out of sight is borne the brave corpse.

4
I turn but do not extricate myself,
Confused, a past-reading, another, but with
    darkness yet.

The beach is cut by the razory ice-wind—the wreck
    guns sound,
The tempest lulls and the moon comes floundering
    through the drifts.

I look where the ship helplessly heads end on—
    I hear the burst as she strikes—I hear the howls
    of dismay, they grow fainter and fainter.

I cannot aid with my wringing fingers,
I can but rush to the surf and let it drench me and
    freeze upon me.

I search with the crowd—not one of the company is
    washed to us alive,
In the morning I help pick up the dead and lay
    them in rows in a barn.

5

Now of the old war-days, the defeat at Brooklyn,
Washington stands inside the lines—he stands on
the entrenched hills amid a crowd of officers,
His face is cold and damp—he cannot repress the
weeping drops, he lifts the glass perpetually to his
eyes—the color is blanched from his cheeks,
He sees the slaughter of the southern braves
confided to him by their parents.

The same at last and at last when peace is declared,
He stands in the room of the old tavern—the
well-beloved soldiers all pass through.

The officers speechless and slow draw near in their
turns,
The chief encircles their necks with his arm and
kisses them on the cheek,
He kisses lightly the wet cheeks one after another,
he shakes hands and bids goodbye to the army.

6

Now I tell what my mother told me today as we sat at
dinner together,
Of when she was a nearly grown girl living home
with her parents on the old homestead.

A red squaw came one breakfast-time to the old
homestead,

On her back she carried a bundle of rushes for
    rush-bottoming chairs;
Her hair straight shiny coarse black and profuse
    half-enveloped her face,
Her step was free and elastic, her voice sounded
    exquisitely as she spoke.

My mother looked in delight and amazement at the
    stranger,
She looked at the freshness of her tall-borne face
    and full and pliant limbs,
The more she looked upon her she loved her,
Never before had she seen such wonderful beauty
    and purity;
She made her sit on a bench by the jamb of the
    fireplace, she cooked food for her,
She had no work to give her but she gave her
    remembrance and fondness.

The red squaw staid all the forenoon, and
    toward the middle of the afternoon she went
    away,
O my mother was loth to have her go away,
All the week she thought of her—she watched for
    her many a month,
She remembered her many a winter and many a
    summer,
But the red squaw never came nor was heard of
    there again.

Now Lucifer was not dead—or if he was I am his
    sorrowful terrible heir,
I have been wronged—I am oppressed—I hate him
    that oppresses me,
I will either destroy him, or he shall release me.

Damn him! how he does defile me,
How he informs against my brother and sister and
    takes pay for their blood,
How he laughs when I look down the bend after the
    steamboat that carries away my woman.

Now the vast dusk bulk that is the whale's bulk, it
    seems mine,
Warily, sportsman! though I lie so sleepy and
    sluggish, my tap is death.

7
A show of the summer softness, a contact of
    something unseen, an amour of the light
    and air,
I am jealous and overwhelmed with friendliness,
And will go gallivant with the light and the air
    myself,
And have an unseen something to be in contact
    with them also.

O love and summer! you are in the dreams and
    in me,

Autumn and winter are in the dreams—the farmer
goes with his thrift,
The droves and crops increase, the barns are
well-filled.

Elements merge in the night—ships make tacks
in the dreams the sailor sails—the exile returns
home,
The fugitive returns unharmed—the immigrant is
back beyond months and years,
The poor Irishman lives in the simple house of his
childhood, with the well-known neighbors and
faces,
They warmly welcome him—he is barefoot again,
he forgets he is well off;
The Dutchman voyages home, and the Scotchman
and Welshman voyage home, and the native of
the Mediterranean voyages home,
To every port of England and France and Spain
enter well-filled ships,
The Swiss foots it toward his hills—the Prussian
goes his way, and the Hungarian his way, and the
Pole goes his way,
The Swede returns, and the Dane and Norwegian
return.

The homeward bound and the outward bound,
The beautiful lost swimmer, the ennuyee, the
onanist, the female that loves unrequited, the
money-maker,

The actor and actress, those through with their
    parts and those waiting to commence,
The affectionate boy, the husband and wife, the
    voter, the nominee that is chosen and the
    nominee that has failed,
The great already known, and the great anytime
    after to day,
The stammerer, the sick, the perfect-formed, the
    homely,
The criminal that stood in the box, the judge that
    sat and sentenced him, the fluent lawyers, the
    jury, the audience,
The laugher and weeper, the dancer, the midnight
    widow, the red squaw,
The consumptive, the erysipalite, the idiot, he that
    is wronged,
The antipodes, and every one between this and
    them in the dark,
I swear they are averaged now—one is no better
    than the other,
The night and sleep have likened them and
    restored them.

I swear they are all beautiful,
Every one that sleeps is beautiful—every thing
    in the dim night is beautiful,
The wildest and bloodiest is over and all is peace.

Peace is always beautiful,
The myth of heaven indicates peace and night.

The myth of heaven indicates the soul,
The soul is always beautiful—it appears more or it
    appears less—it comes or lags behind,
It comes from its enbowered garden and looks
    pleasantly on itself and encloses the world,
Perfect and clean the genitals previously jetting, and
    perfect and clean the womb cohering,
The head well-grown and proportioned and plumb,
    and the bowels and joints proportioned and
    plumb.

The soul is always beautiful,
The universe is duly in order, every thing is in its
    place,
What is arrived is in its place, and what waits is in its
    place,
The twisted skull waits, the watery or rotten blood
    waits,
The child of the glutton or venerealee waits long,
    and the child of the drunkard waits long, and the
    drunkard himself waits long,
The sleepers that lived and died wait—the far
    advanced are to go on in their turns, and the far
    behind are to go on in their turns,
The diverse shall be no less diverse, but they shall
    flow and unite—they unite now.

8

The sleepers are very beautiful as they lie unclothed,
They flow hand in hand over the whole earth from
    east to west as they lie unclothed,
The Asiatic and African are hand in hand—the
    European and American are hand in hand,
Learned and unlearned are hand in hand—and
    male and female are hand in hand,
The bare arm of the girl crosses the bare breast of
    her lover—they press close without lust—his lips
    press her neck,
The father holds his grown or ungrown son in his
    arms with measureless love, and the son holds
    the father in his arms with measureless love,
The white hair of the mother shines on the white
    wrist of the daughter,
The breath of the boy goes with the breath of the
    man, friend is inarmed by friend,
The scholar kisses the teacher and the teacher kisses
    the scholar—the wronged is made right,
The call of the slave is one with the master's call,
    and the master salutes the slave,
The felon steps forth from the prison—the insane
    becomes sane—the suffering of sick persons is
    relieved,
The sweatings and fevers stop, the throat that was
    unsound is sound, the lungs of the consumptive
    are resumed, the poor distressed head is free,
The joints of the rheumatic move as smoothly as
    ever, and smoother than ever,

Stiflings and passages open—the paralysed become
    supple,
The swelled and convulsed and congested awake to
    themselves in condition,
They pass the invigoration of the night and the
    chemistry of the night and awake.

I too pass from the night,
I stay awhile away O night, but I return to you again
    and love you.

Why should I be afraid to trust myself to you?
I am not afraid, I have been well brought forward
    by you,
I love the rich running day, but I do not desert her
    in whom I lay so long,
I know not how I came of you, and I know not
    where I go with you—but I know I came well and
    shall go well.

I will stop only a time with the night, and rise
    betimes,
I will duly pass the day O my mother and duly
    return to you.

Poem of the Body

1

The bodies of men and women engirth me, and I
     engirth them,
They will not let me off nor I them till I go with
     them and respond to them and love them.

Was it doubted if those who corrupt their own live
     bodies conceal themselves?
And if those who defile the living are as bad as they
     who defile the dead?

2

The expression of the body of man or woman balks
     account,
The male is perfect and that of the female is
     perfect.

The expression of a well-made man appears not
     only in his face,
It is in his limbs and joints also, it is curiously in the
     joints of his hips and wrists,
It is in his walk, the carriage of his neck, the flex of
     his waist and knees—dress does not hide him,
The strong sweet supple quality he has strikes
     through the cotton and flannel,
To see him pass conveys as much as the best poem,
     perhaps more,

You linger to see his back and the back of his neck
and shoulder-side.

The sprawl and fulness of babes, the bosoms and
heads of women, the folds of their dress, their
style as we pass in the street, the contour of their
shape downwards,
The swimmer naked in the swimming-bath, seen
as he swims through the salt transparent green-
shine, or lies on his back and rolls silently with
the heave of the water,
Framers bare-armed framing a house, hoisting the
beams in their places, or using the mallet and
mortising-chisel,
The bending forward and backward of rowers in
row-boats — the horseman in his saddle,
Girls and mothers and housekeepers in all their
exquisite offices,
The group of laborers seated at noon-time with
their open dinner-kettles, and their wives waiting,
The female soothing a child — the farmer's
daughter in the garden or cow-yard,
The young fellow hoeing corn — the sleigh-driver
guiding his six horses through the crowd,
The wrestle of wrestlers, two apprentice-boys, quite
grown, lusty, good-natured, native-born, out on
the vacant lot at sun-down after work,
The coats vests and caps thrown down, the embrace
of love and resistance,

The upper-hold and under-hold—the hair rumpled
    over and blinding the eyes,
The march of firemen in their own costumes—
    the play of the masculine muscle through
    clean-setting trowsers and waist-straps,
The slow return from the fire, the pause when the
    bell strikes suddenly again—the listening on the
    alert,
The natural perfect and varied attitudes—the bent
    head, the curved neck, the counting:
Such-like I love—I loosen myself and pass freely—
    and am at the mother's breast with the little
    child,
And swim with the swimmer, and wrestle with the
    wrestlers, and march in line with the firemen,
    and pause and listen and count.

3
I knew a man—he was a common farmer—he was
    the father of five sons—and in them were the
    fathers of sons—and in them were the fathers of
    sons.

This man was a wonderful vigor and calmness and
    beauty of person,
The shape of his head, the richness and breadth
    of his manners, the pale yellow and white of his
    hair and beard, the immeasurable meaning of his
    black eyes,

These I used to go and visit him to see—he was wise
    also,
He was six feet tall—he was over eighty years old—
    his sons were massive clean bearded tan-faced
    and handsome,
They and his daughters loved him—all who saw
    him loved him—they did not love him by
    allowance—they loved him with personal
    love,
He drank water only—the blood showed like
    scarlet through the clear-brown skin of his face,
He was a frequent gunner and fisher—he sailed
    his boat himself—he had a fine one presented
    to him by a ship-joiner—he had fowling-pieces,
    presented to him by men that loved him,
When he went with his five sons and many grand-
    sons to hunt or fish you would pick him out as
    the most beautiful and vigorous of the gang,
You would wish long and long to be with him—you
    would wish to sit by him in the boat that you and
    he might touch each other.

4
I have perceived that to be with those I like is
    enough,
To stop in company with the rest at evening is
    enough,
To be surrounded by beautiful curious breathing
    laughing flesh is enough,

To pass among them, to touch any one, to rest my
　　arm ever so lightly round his or her neck for a
　　moment—what is this then?

I do not ask any more delight—I swim in it as in
　　a sea.

There is something in staying close to men and
　　women and looking on them and in the contact
　　and odor of them that pleases the soul well,
All things please the soul, but these please the soul
　　well.

5
This is the female form,
A divine nimbus exhales from it from head to foot,
It attracts with fierce undeniable attraction,
I am drawn by its breath as if I were no more than a
　　helpless vapor—all falls aside but myself and it,
Books, art, religion, time, the visible and solid earth,
　　the atmosphere and the fringed clouds, what
　　was expected of heaven or feared of hell are now
　　consumed,
Mad filaments, ungovernable shoots play out of it,
　　the response likewise ungovernable,
Hair, bosom, hips, bend of legs, negligent falling
　　hands—all diffused—mine too diffused,
Ebb stung by the flow, and flow stung by the ebb—
　　love-flesh swelling and deliciously aching,

Limitless limpid jets of love hot and enormous,
　　quivering jelly of love, white-blow and delirious
　　juice,
Bridegroom night of love working surely and softly
　　into the prostrate dawn,
Undulating into the willing and yielding day,
Lost in the cleave of the clasping and sweet-fleshed
　　day.

This is the nucleus—after the child is born of
　　woman the man is born of woman,
This is the bath of birth—this is the merge of small
　　and large and the outlet again.

Be not ashamed women—your privilege encloses
　　the rest, it is the exit of the rest,
You are the gates of the body and you are the gates
　　of the soul.

The female contains all qualities and tempers
　　them—she is in her place—she moves with
　　perfect balance,
She is all things duly veiled—she is both passive and
　　active—she is to conceive daughters as well as
　　sons and sons as well as daughters.

As I see my soul reflected in nature, as I see through
　　a mist one with inexpressible completeness and
　　beauty, see the bent head and arms folded over
　　the breast—the female I see.

6

The male is not less the soul, nor more—he too is
    in his place,
He too is all qualities—he is action and power—the
    flush of the known universe is in him,
Scorn becomes him well and appetite and defiance
    become him well,
The fiercest largest passions, a bliss that is
    utmost and sorrow that is utmost become him
    well—pride is for him,
The full-spread pride of man is calming and
    excellent to the soul,
Knowledge becomes him—he likes it always—he
    brings everything to the test of himself,
Whatever the survey, whatever the sea and the sail,
    he strikes soundings at last only here,
Where else does he strike soundings except here?

The man's body is sacred and the woman's body is
    sacred, it is no matter who,
Is it a slave? Is it one of the dull-faced immigrants
    just landed on the wharf?

Each belongs here or anywhere just as much as the
    well-off—just as much as you,
Each has his or her place in the procession.

All is a procession,
The universe is a procession with measured and
    perfect motion.

Do you know so much yourself that you call the
     slave or the dull-face ignorant?
Do you suppose you have a right to a good sight,
     and he or she has no right to a sight?
Do you think matter has cohered together from its
     diffused float, and the soil is on the surface and
     water runs and vegetation sprouts for you only,
     and not for him and her?

7
A slave at auction!
I help the auctioneer—the sloven does not half
     know his business.

Gentlemen look on this curious creature,
Whatever the bids of the bidders they cannot be
     high enough for him,
For him the globe lay preparing quintillions of years
     without one animal or plant,
For him the revolving cycles truly and steadily
     rolled.

In this head the all-baffling brain,
In it and below it the making of the attributes of
     heroes.

Examine these limbs, red black or white—they are
     very cunning in tendon and nerve,
They shall be stript that you may see them.

Exquisite senses, life-lit eyes, pluck, volition,
Flakes of breast-muscle, pliant backbone and neck,
    flesh not flabby, good-sized arms and legs,
And wonders within there yet.

Within there runs his blood, the same old blood,
    the same red running blood,
There swells and jets his heart—there all passions
    and desires—all reachings and aspirations,
Do you think they are not there because they are
    not expressed in parlors and lecture-rooms?

This is not only one man, he is the father of those
    who shall be fathers in their turns,
In him the start of populous states and rich
    republics,
Of him countless immortal lives with countless
    embodiments and enjoyments.

How do you know who shall come from the
    offspring of his offspring through the centuries?
Who might you find you have come from yourself if
    you could trace back through the centuries?

8
A woman at auction,
She too is not only herself—she is the teeming
    mother of mothers,
She is the bearer of them that shall grow and be
    mates to the mothers.

Her daughters or their daughters' daughters—who
  knows who shall mate with them?
Who knows through the centuries what heroes may
  come from them?

In them and of them natal love—in them the divine
  mystery—the same old beautiful mystery.

Have you ever loved a woman?
Your mother—is she living? have you been much
  with her? and has she been much with you?
Do you not see that these are exactly the same to all
  in all nations and times all over the earth?

If life and the soul are sacred the human body is
  sacred,
And the glory and sweet of a man is the token of
  manhood untainted,
And in man or woman a clean strong firm-fibred
  body is beautiful as the most beautiful face.

Have you seen the fool that corrupted his own live
  body? or the fool that corrupted her own live
  body?
For they do not conceal themselves, and cannot
  conceal themselves.

Who degrades or defiles the living human body is
  cursed,

Who degrades or defiles the body of the dead is not
    more cursed.

9
O my body! I dare not desert the likes of you in
    other men and women, nor the likes of the parts
    of you;
I believe the likes of you are to stand or fall with the
    likes of the soul, (and that they are the soul,)
I believe the likes of you shall stand or fall with my
    poems—and that they are poems,
Man's, woman's, child's, youth's, wife's, husband's,
    mother's, father's, young man's, young woman's
    poems,
Head, neck, hair, ears, drop and tympan of the ears,
Eyes, eye-fringes, iris of the eye, eye-brows, and the
    waking or sleeping of the lids,
Mouth, tongue, lips, teeth, roof of the mouth, jaws,
    and the jaw-hinges,
Nose, nostrils of the nose, and the partition,
Cheeks, temples, forehead, chin, throat, back of the
    neck, neck-slue,
Strong shoulders, manly beard, scapula, hind-
    shoulders, and the ample side-round of the
    chest,
Upper-arm, arm-pit, elbow-socket, lower-arm,
    arm-sinews, arm-bones,
Wrist and wrist-joints, hand, palm, knuckles,
    thumb, fore-finger, finger-balls, finger-joints,
    finger-nails,

Broad breast-front, curling hair of the breast, breast-
bone, breast-side,
Ribs, belly, back-bone, joints of the back-bone,
Hips, hip-sockets, hip-strength, inward and outward
round, man-balls, man-root,
Strong set of thighs, well carrying the trunk above,
Leg-fibres, knee, knee-pan, upper-leg, under-leg,
Ankles, instep, foot-ball, toes, toe-joints, the heel,
All attitudes, all the shapeliness, all the belongings
of my or your body, or of any one's body, male or
female,
The lung-sponges, the stomach-sac, the bowels sweet
and clean,
The brain in its folds inside the skull-frame,
Sympathies, heart-valves, palate-valves, sexuality,
maternity,
Womanhood, and all that is a woman — and the
man that comes from woman,
The womb, the teats, nipples, breast-milk, tears,
laughter, weeping, love-looks, love-perturbations
and risings,
The voice, articulation, language, whispering,
shouting aloud,
Food, drink, pulse, digestion, sweat, sleep, walking,
swimming,
Poise on the hips, leaping, reclining, embracing,
arm-curving, and tightening,
The continual changes of the flex of the mouth,
and around the eyes,
The skin, the sun-burnt shade, freckles, hair,

The curious sympathy one feels, when feeling with
the hand the naked meat of his own body, or
another person's body,
The circling rivers, the breath, and breathing it in
and out,
The beauty of the waist, and thence of the hips, and
thence downward toward the knees,
The thin red jellies within you, or within me — the
bones, and the marrow in the bones,
The exquisite realization of health,
O I think now these are not the parts and poems of
the body only, but of the soul,
O I think these are the soul!

There Was a Child Went Forth

There was a child went forth every day,
And the first object he looked upon, that object he
became,
And that object became part of him for the day or
a certain part of the day, or for many years or
stretching cycles of years.

The early lilacs became part of this child,
And grass, and white and red morning-glories,
and white and red clover, and the song of the
phœbe-bird,
And the March-born lambs, and the sow's pink-faint
litter, and the mare's foal, and the cow's calf,

and the noisy brood of the barnyard or by the
mire of the pond-side, and the fish suspending
themselves so curiously below there, and the
beautiful curious liquid, and the water-plants with
their graceful flat heads, all became part of him.

And the field-sprouts of April and May became part
of him, winter-grain sprouts, and those of the
light-yellow corn, and of the esculent roots of the
garden,
And the apple-trees covered with blossoms, and
the fruit afterward, and wood-berries, and the
commonest weeds by the road,
And the old drunkard staggering home from the
outhouse of the tavern whence he had lately
risen,
And the schoolmistress that passed on her way to
the school, and the friendly boys that passed, and
the quarrelsome boys, and the tidy and fresh-
cheeked girls, and the barefoot negro boy and
girl,
And all the changes of city and country wherever he
went.

His own parents, he that had propelled the father-
stuff at night and fathered him, and she that
conceived him in her womb and birthed him,
they gave this child more of themselves than that,
They gave him afterward every day—they and of
them became part of him.

The mother at home quietly placing the dishes on
the supper-table,
The mother with mild words—clean her cap and
gown, a wholesome odor falling off her person
and clothes as she walks by,
The father, strong, self-sufficient, manly, mean,
angered, unjust,
The blow, the quick loud word, the tight bargain,
the crafty lure,
The family usages, the language, the company, the
furniture—the yearning and swelling heart,
Affection that will not be gainsayed—the sense of
what is real—the thought if after all it should
prove unreal,
The doubts of day-time and the doubts of
night-time—the curious whether and how,
Whether that which appears so is so, or is it all
flashes and specks?
Men and women crowding fast in the streets—if
they are not flashes and specks what are they?
The streets themselves, and the facades of houses,
the goods in the windows,
Vehicles, teams, the tiered wharves—and the huge
crossing at the ferries,
The village on the highland seen from afar at
sunset—the river between,
Shadows, aureola and mist, light falling on roofs
and gables of white or brown, three miles off,
The schooner near by sleepily dropping down the
tide—the little boat slack-towed astern,

The hurrying tumbling waves and quick-broken
    crests and slapping,
The strata of colored clouds, the long bar of
    maroon-tint away solitary by itself—the spread of
    purity it lies motionless in,
The horizon's edge, the flying sea-crow, the
    fragrance of saltmarsh and shore mud,
These became part of that child who went forth
    every day, and who now goes and will always go
    forth every day.

Crossing Brooklyn Ferry

1

Flood-tide below me! I see you, face to face!
Clouds of the west! sun there half an hour high! I
    see you also face to face.

Crowds of men and women attired in the usual
    costumes! how curious you are to me!
On the ferry-boats, the hundreds and hundreds that
    cross, returning home, are more curious to me
    than you suppose,
And you that shall cross from shore to shore
    years hence, are more to me, and more in my
    meditations, than you might suppose.

2

The impalpable sustenance of me from all things, at
   all hours of the day,
The simple, compact, well-joined scheme—myself
   disintegrated, every one disintegrated, yet part of
   the scheme,
The similitudes of the past, and those of the future,
The glories strung like beads on my smallest sights
   and hearings—on the walk in the street, and the
   passage over the river,
The current rushing so swiftly, and swimming with
   me far away,
The others that are to follow me, the ties between
   me and them,
The certainty of others—the life, love, sight,
   hearing of others.

Others will enter the gates of the ferry, and cross
   from shore to shore,
Others will watch the run of the flood-tide,
Others will see the shipping of Manhattan north
   and west, and the heights of Brooklyn to the
   south and east,
Others will see the islands large and small,
Fifty years hence, others will see them as they cross,
   the sun half an hour high,
A hundred years hence, or ever so many hundred
   years hence, others will see them,
Will enjoy the sunset, the pouring-in of the flood-
   tide, the falling-back to the sea of the ebb-tide.

3

It avails not, neither time or place—distance
   avails not,
I am with you, you men and women of a generation,
   or ever so many generations hence,
Just as you feel when you look on the river and sky,
   so I felt,
Just as any of you is one of a living crowd, I was one
   of a crowd,
Just as you are refreshed by the gladness of the river,
   and the bright flow, I was refreshed,
Just as you stand and lean on the rail, yet hurry with
   the swift current, I stood, yet was hurried,
Just as you look on the numberless masts of ships,
   and the thick-stemmed pipes of steamboats, I
   looked.

I too many and many a time crossed the river of old,
Watched the December sea-gulls—saw them high in
   the air, floating with motionless wings, oscillating
   their bodies,
Saw how the glistening yellow lit up parts of their
   bodies, and left the rest in strong shadow,
Saw the slow-wheeling circles, and the gradual
   edging toward the south,
Saw the reflection of the summer sky in the water,
Had my eyes dazzled by the shimmering track of
   beams,
Looked at the fine centrifugal spokes of light round
   the shape of my head in the sunlit water,

Looked on the haze on the hills southward and
south-westward,
Looked on the vapor as it flew in fleeces tinged with
violet,
Looked toward the lower bay to notice the arriving
ships,
Saw their approach, saw aboard those that were
near me,
Saw the white sails of schooners and sloops, saw the
ships at anchor,
The sailors at work in the rigging, or out astride the
spars,
The round masts, the swinging motion of the hulls,
the slender serpentine pennants,
The large and small steamers in motion, the pilots
in their pilot-houses,
The white wake left by the passage, the quick
tremulous whirl of the wheels,
The flags of all nations, the falling of them at
sunset,
The scallop-edged waves in the twilight, the ladled
cups, the frolicsome crests and glistening,
The stretch afar growing dimmer and dimmer, the
gray walls of the granite storehouses by the docks,
On the river the shadowy group, the big steam-tug
closely flanked on each side by the barges—the
hay-boat, the belated lighter,
On the neighboring shore, the fires from the
foundry chimneys burning high and glaringly
into the night,

Casting their flicker of black, contrasted with wild
     red and yellow light, over the tops of houses, and
     down into the clefts of streets.

4
These, and all else, were to me the same as they are
     to you,
I loved well those cities,
I loved well the stately and rapid river,
The men and women I saw were all near to me,
Others the same—others who look back on me,
     because I looked forward to them,
(The time will come, though I stop here to-day and
     to-night.)

5
What is it, then, between us?
What is the count of the scores or hundreds of years
     between us?

Whatever it is, it avails not—distance avails not, and
     place avails not.

I too lived, Brooklyn of ample hills was mine,
I too walked the streets of Manhattan island, and
     bathed in the waters around it,
I too felt the curious abrupt questionings stir
     within me,
In the day, among crowds of people, sometimes they
     came upon me,

In my walks home late at night, or as I lay in my bed,
    they came upon me,
I too had been struck from the float forever held in
    solution,
I too had received identity by my body,
That I was, I knew was of my body—and what I
    should be, I knew I should be of my body.

6
It is not upon you alone the dark patches fall,
The dark threw patches down upon me also,
The best I had done seemed to me blank and
    suspicious,
My great thoughts, as I supposed them, were they
    not in reality meagre?
Nor is it you alone who know what it is to be evil,
I am he who knew what it was to be evil,
I too knitted the old knot of contrariety,
Blabbed, blushed, resented, lied, stole, grudged,
Had guile, anger, lust, hot wishes I dared not
    speak,
Was wayward, vain, greedy, shallow, sly, a solitary
    committer, a coward, a malignant person,
The wolf, the snake, the hog, not wanting in me,
The cheating look, the frivolous word, the
    adulterous wish, not wanting,
Refusals, hates, postponements, meanness, laziness,
    none of these wanting,
Was one with the rest, the days and haps of the
    rest,

Was called by my nighest name by clear loud voices
    of young men as they saw me approaching or
    passing,
Felt their arms on my neck as I stood, or the
    negligent leaning of their flesh against me as
    I sat,
Saw many I loved in the street, or ferry-boat, or
    public assembly, yet never told them a word,
Lived the same life with the rest, the same old
    laughing, gnawing, sleeping,
Played the part that still looks back on the actor or
    actress,
The same old role, the role that is what we make it,
    as great as we like,
Or as small as we like, or both great and small.

7
Closer yet I approach you,
What thought you have of me, I had as much of
    you — I laid in my stores in advance,
I considered long and seriously of you before you
    were born.

Who was to know what should come home to me?
Who knows but I am enjoying this?
Who knows, for all the distance, but I am as good as
    looking at you now, for all you cannot see me?

8

Ah, what can ever be more stately and admirable to
    me than my mast-hemm'd Manhattan,
My river and sunset, and my scallop-edged waves of
    flood-tide,
The sea-gulls oscillating their bodies, the hay-boat in
    the twilight, and the belated lighter;
What gods can exceed these that clasp me by the
    hand, and with voices I love call me promptly and
    loudly by my nighest name as I approach?
What is more subtle than this which ties me to the
    woman or man that looks in my face,
Which fuses me into you now, and pours my
    meaning into you?

We understand, then, do we not?
What I promised without mentioning it, have you
    not accepted?
What the study could not teach—what the
    preaching could not accomplish is accomplished,
    is it not?

9

Flow on, river! flow with the flood-tide, and ebb with
    the ebb-tide!
Frolic on, crested and scallop-edged waves!
Gorgeous clouds of the sunset! drench with your
    splendor me, or the men and women generations
    after me!

Cross from shore to shore, countless crowds of
    passengers!
Stand up, tall masts of Mannahatta!—stand up,
    beautiful hills of Brooklyn!
Throb, baffled and curious brain! throw out
    questions and answers!
Suspend here and everywhere, eternal float of
    solution!
Blab, blush, lie, steal, you or I or any one after us!
Gaze, loving and thirsting eyes, in the house, or
    street, or public assembly!
Sound out, voices of young men! loudly and
    musically call me by my nighest name!
Live, old life! play the part that looks back on the
    actor or actress!
Play the old role, the role that is great or small,
    according as one makes it!
Consider, you who peruse me, whether I may not in
    unknown ways be looking upon you!
Be firm, rail over the river, to support those who
    lean idly, yet haste with the hasting current!
Fly on, sea-birds! fly sideways, or wheel in large
    circles high in the air!
Receive the summer-sky, you water! and faithfully
    hold it, till all downcast eyes have time to take it
    from you!
Diverge, fine spokes of light, from the shape of my
    head, or any one's head, in the sun-lit water!
Come on, ships from the lower bay! pass up or
    down, white-sailed schooners, sloops, lighters!

Flaunt away, flags of all nations! be duly lowered at
    sunset!
Burn high your fires, foundry chimneys! cast black
    shadows at nightfall! cast red and yellow light
    over the tops of the houses!
Appearances, now or henceforth, indicate what
    you are,
You necessary film, continue to envelop the soul,
About my body for me, and your body for you, be
    hung our divinest aromas,
Thrive, cities! bring your freight, bring your shows,
    ample and sufficient rivers,
Expand, being than which none else is perhaps
    more spiritual,
Keep your places, objects than which none else is
    more lasting.

You have waited, you always wait, you dumb,
    beautiful ministers,
We receive you with free sense at last, and are
    insatiate henceforward,
Not you any more shall be able to foil us, or
    withhold yourselves from us,
We use you, and do not cast you aside—we plant
    you permanently within us,
We fathom you not—we love you—there is
    perfection in you also,
You furnish your parts toward eternity,
Great or small, you furnish your parts toward the
    soul.

Poem of the Proposition of Nakedness

Respondez! Respondez!

Let every one answer! let those who sleep be waked!
let none evade!

Must we still go on with our affectations and
sneaking?

Let me bring this to a close—I pronounce openly
for a new distribution of roles,

Let that which stood in front go behind! and let
that which was behind advance to the front and
speak!

Let murderers, thieves, bigots, fools, unclean
persons, offer new propositions!

Let the old propositions be postponed!

Let faces and theories be turned inside out! let
meanings be freely criminal, as well as results!
(Say! can results be criminal, and meanings not
criminal?)

Let there be no suggestion above the suggestion of
drudgery!

Let none be pointed toward his destination! (Say!
do you know your destination?)

Let men and women be mocked with bodies and
mocked with souls!

Let the love that waits in them, wait! let it die, or
pass still-born to other spheres!

Let the sympathy that waits in every man, wait! or let
it also pass, a dwarf, to other spheres!

Let contradictions prevail! let one thing contradict

another! and let one line of my poems contradict
   another!
Let the people sprawl with yearning aimless hands!
   let their tongues be broken! let their eyes be
   discouraged! let none descend into their hearts
   with the fresh lusciousness of love!
Let the theory of America be management, caste,
   comparison! (Say! what other theory would you?)
Let them that distrust birth and death lead the rest!
   (Say! why shall they not lead you?)
Let the crust of hell be neared and trod on! let the
   days be darker than the nights! let slumber bring
   less slumber than waking-time brings!
Let the world never appear to him or her for whom
   it was all made!
Let the heart of the young man exile itself from the
   heart of the old man! and let the heart of the old
   man be exiled from that of the young man!
Let the sun and moon go! let scenery take the
   applause of the audience! let there be apathy
   under the stars!
Let freedom prove no man's inalienable right! every
   one who can tyrannize, let him tyrannize to his
   satisfaction!
Let none but infidels be countenanced!
Let the eminence of meanness, treachery,
   sarcasm, hate, greed, indecency, impotence,
   lust, be taken for granted above all! let writers,
   judges, governments, households, religions,
   philosophies, take such for granted above all!

Let the worst men beget children out of the worst
  women!
Let priests still play at immortality!
Let Death be inaugurated!
Let nothing remain upon the earth except the ashes
  of teachers, artists, moralists, lawyers, and learned
  and polite persons!
Let him who is without my poems be assassinated!
Let the cow, the horse, the camel, the garden-bee—
  let the mud-fish, the lobster, the mussel, eel, the
  sting-ray, and the grunting pig-fish—let these,
  and the like of these, be put on a perfect equality
  with man and woman!
Let churches accommodate serpents, vermin, and
  the corpses of those who have died of the most
  filthy of diseases!
Let marriage slip down among fools, and be for
  none but fools!
Let men among themselves talk and think obscenely
  of women! and let women among themselves talk
  and think obscenely of men!
Let every man doubt every woman! and let every
  woman trick every man!
Let us all, without missing one, be exposed in public
  naked, monthly, at the peril of our lives! let
  our bodies be freely handled and examined by
  whoever chooses!
Let nothing but copies at second hand be permitted
  to exist upon the earth!

Let the earth desert God, nor let there ever
   henceforth be mentioned the name of God!
Let there be no God!
Let there be money, business, imports, exports,
   custom, authority, precedents, pallor, dyspepsia,
   smut, ignorance, unbelief!
Let judges and criminals be transposed! let the
   prison-keepers be put in prison! let those that
   were prisoners take the keys! (Say! why might
   they not just as well be transposed?)
Let the slaves be masters! Let the masters become
   slaves!
Let the reformers descend from the stands where
   they are forever bawling! let an idiot or insane
   person appear on each of the stands!
Let the Asiatic, the African, the European, the
   American and the Australian, go armed against
   the murderous stealthiness of each other! let
   them sleep armed! let none believe in good-will!
Let there be no living wisdom! let such be scorned
   and derided off from the earth!
Let a floating cloud in the sky—let a wave of the
   sea—let one glimpse of your eye-sight upon the
   landscape or grass—let growing mint, spinach,
   onions, tomatoes—let these be exhibited as
   shows at a great price for admission!
Let all the men of These States stand aside for a few
   smouchers! let the few seize on what they choose!
   let the rest gawk, giggle, starve, obey!

Let shadows be furnished with genitals! let
    substances be deprived of their genitals!
Let there be wealthy and immense cities—but
    through any of them, not a single poet, saviour,
    knower, lover!
Let the infidels of These States laugh all faith away!
    if one man be found who has faith, let the rest
    set upon him! let them affright faith! let them
    destroy the power of breeding faith!
Let the she-harlots and the he-harlots be prudent!
    Let them dance on, while seeming lasts!
    (O seeming! seeming! seeming!)
Let the preachers recite creeds! Let them still teach
    only what they have been taught!
Let the preacher of creeds never dare to go
    meditate upon the hills, alone, by day or by
    night! (If one ever once dare, he is lost!)
Let insanity have charge of sanity!
Let books take the place of trees, animals, rivers,
    clouds!
Let the daubed portraits of heroes supersede heroes!
Let the manhood of man never take steps after
    itself! let it take steps after eunuchs, and after
    consumptive and genteel persons!
Let the white person tread the black person under
    his heel! (Say! which is trodden under heel,
    after all?)
Let the reflections of the things of the world be
    studied in mirrors! let the things themselves
    continue unstudied!

Let a man seek pleasure everywhere except in
  himself! let a woman seek happiness everywhere
  except in herself! (What real happiness have you
  had one single hour through your whole life?)
Let the limited years of life do nothing for the
  limitless years of death! (What do you suppose
  death will do, then?)

Out of the Cradle Endlessly Rocking

Out of the cradle endlessly rocking,
Out of the mocking-bird's throat, the musical
  shuttle,
Out of the Ninth-month midnight,
Over the sterile sands, and the fields beyond, where
  the child, leaving his bed, wandered alone,
  bareheaded, barefoot,
Down from the showered halo,
Up from the mystic play of shadows, twining and
  twisting as if they were alive,
Out from the patches of briers and blackberries,
From the memories of the bird that chanted
  to me,
From your memories, sad brother—from the fitful
  risings and fallings I heard,
From under that yellow half-moon, late-risen, and
  swollen as if with tears,
From those beginning notes of sickness and love,
  there in the transparent mist,

From the thousand responses of my heart, never
    to cease,
From the myriad thence-aroused words,
From the word stronger and more delicious
    than any,
From such, as now they start, the scene revisiting,
As a flock, twittering, rising, or overhead passing,
Borne hither—ere all eludes me, hurriedly,
A man—yet by these tears a little boy again,
Throwing myself on the sand, confronting the waves,
I, chanter of pains and joys, uniter of here and
    hereafter,
Taking all hints to use them—but swiftly leaping
    beyond them,
A reminiscence sing.

Once, Paumanok,
When the snows had melted—when the lilac-scent
    was in the air, and the Fifth-month grass was
    growing,
Up this seashore, in some briers,
Two guests from Alabama—two together,
And their nest, and four light-green eggs, spotted
    with brown,
And every day the he-bird, to and fro, near at hand,
And every day the she-bird, crouched on her nest,
    silent, with bright eyes,
And every day I, a curious boy, never too close,
    never disturbing them,
Cautiously peering, absorbing, translating.

Shine! shine!
Pour down your warmth, great sun!
While we bask — we two together.

Two together!
Winds blow south, or winds blow north,
Day come white, or night come black,
Home, or rivers and mountains from home,
Singing all time, minding no time,
If we two but keep together.

Till of a sudden,
May-be killed, unknown to her mate,
One forenoon the she-bird crouched not on the
    nest,
Nor returned that afternoon, nor the next,
Nor ever appeared again.

And thenceforward, all summer, in the sound of
    the sea,
And at night, under the full of the moon, in calmer
    weather,
Over the hoarse surging of the sea,
Or flitting from brier to brier by day,
I saw, I heard at intervals, the remaining one, the
    he-bird,
The solitary guest from Alabama.

Blow! blow!
Blow up sea-winds along Paumanok's shore;
I wait and I wait, till you blow my mate to me.

Yes, when the stars glistened,
All night long, on the prong of a moss-scallop'd
  stake,
Down, almost amid the slapping waves,
Sat the lone singer, wonderful, causing tears.

He called on his mate,
He poured forth the meanings which I, of all men,
  know.

Yes, my brother, I know,
The rest might not—but I have treasured every
  note,
For once, and more than once, dimly, down to the
  beach gliding,
Silent, avoiding the moonbeams, blending myself
  with the shadows,
Recalling now the obscure shapes, the echoes, the
  sounds and sights after their sorts,
The white arms out in the breakers tirelessly tossing,
I, with bare feet, a child, the wind wafting my hair,
Listened long and long.

Listened, to keep, to sing—now translating the
  notes,
Following you, my brother.

Soothe! soothe!
Close on its wave soothes the wave behind,

And again another behind, embracing and lapping, every
  one close,
But my love soothes not me.

Low hangs the moon—it rose late,
O it is lagging—O I think it is heavy with love.

O madly the sea pushes upon the land,
With love—with love.

O night! O do I not see my love fluttering out there among
  the breakers?
What is that little black thing I see there in the white?

Loud! loud!
Loud I call to you my love!
High and clear I shoot my voice over the waves,
Surely you must know who is here,
You must know who I am, my love.

Low-hanging moon!
What is that dusky spot in your brown yellow?
O it is the shape of my mate!
O moon, do not keep her from me any longer.

Land! O land!
Whichever way I turn, O I think you could give me my
  mate back again, if you would,
For I am almost sure I see her dimly whichever way I look.

O rising stars!
Perhaps the one I want so much will rise with some
   of you.

O throat!
Sound clearer through the atmosphere!
Pierce the woods, the earth,
Somewhere listening to catch you must be the one I want.

Shake out, carols!
Solitary here — the night's carols!
Carols of lonesome love! death's carols!
Carols under that lagging, yellow, waning moon!
O under that moon, where she droops almost down into
   the sea!
O reckless, despairing carols.

But soft! sink low — soft!
Soft! let me just murmur,
And do you wait a moment, you husky-noised sea,
For somewhere I believe I heard my mate responding to me,
So faint — I must be still to listen,
But not altogether still, for then she might not come
   immediately to me.

Hither, my love!
Here I am! here!
With this just-sustained note I announce myself to you,
This gentle call is for you, my love.

Do not be decoyed elsewhere!
That is the whistle of the wind—it is not my voice,
That is the fluttering of the spray,
Those are the shadows of leaves.

O darkness! O in vain!
O I am very sick and sorrowful.

O brown halo in the sky, near the moon, drooping upon
    the sea!
O troubled reflection in the sea!
O throat! O throbbing heart!
O all—and I singing uselessly all the night.

Murmur! murmur on!
O murmurs—you yourselves make me continue to sing,
    I know not why.
O past! O joy!
In the air—in the woods—over fields,
Loved! loved! loved! loved! loved!
Loved—but no more with me,
We two together no more.

The aria sinking,
All else continuing—the stars shining,
The winds blowing—the notes of the wondrous
    bird echoing,
With angry moans the fierce old mother yet, as ever,
    incessantly moaning,

On the sands of Paumanok's shore gray and
    rustling,
The yellow half-moon, enlarged, sagging
    down, drooping, the face of the sea almost
    touching,
The boy ecstatic—with his bare feet the waves,
    with his hair the atmosphere dallying,
The love in the heart pent, now loose, now at last
    tumultuously bursting,
The aria's meaning, the ears, the soul, swiftly
    depositing,
The strange tears down the cheeks coursing,
The colloquy there—the trio—each uttering,
The undertone—the savage old mother, incessantly
    crying,
To the boy's soul's questions sullenly timing—some
    drowned secret hissing,
To the outsetting bard of love.

Bird! (then said the boy's soul,)
Is it indeed toward your mate you sing? or is it
    mostly to me?
For I that was a child, my tongue's use sleeping,
    now that I have heard you,
Now in a moment I know what I am for—I awake,
And already a thousand singers—a thousand
    songs, clearer, louder, more sorrowful than
    yours,
A thousand warbling echoes have started to life
    within me, never to die.

O throes!

O you demon, singing by yourself—projecting me,

O solitary me, listening—never more shall I cease imitating, perpetuating you,

Never more shall I escape, never more shall the reverberations,

Never more the cries of unsatisfied love be absent from me,

Never again leave me to be the peaceful child I was before what there, in the night,

By the sea, under the yellow and sagging moon,

The dusky demon aroused—the fire, the sweet hell within,

The unknown want, the destiny of me.

O give me some clew!

O if I am to have so much, let me have more!

O a word! O what is my destination?

I fear it is henceforth chaos!

O how joys, dreads, convolutions, human shapes, and all shapes, spring as from graves around me!

O phantoms! you cover all the land, and all the sea!

O I cannot see in the dimness whether you smile or frown upon me;

O vapor, a look, a word! O well-beloved!

O you dear women's and men's phantoms!

A word then, (for I will conquer it,)

The word final, superior to all,

Subtle, sent up—what is it?—I listen;

Are you whispering it, and have been all the time,
  you sea-waves?
Is that it from your liquid rims and wet sands?

Answering, the sea,
Delaying not, hurrying not,
Whispered me through the night, and very plainly
  before daybreak,
Lisped to me constantly the low and delicious word
  death,
And again death—death, death, death,
Hissing melodious, neither like the bird, nor like
  my aroused child's heart,
But edging near, as privately for me, rustling at my
  feet,
And creeping thence steadily up to my ears,
Death, death, death, death, death.

Which I do not forget,
But fuse the song of two together,
That was sung to me in the moonlight on
  Paumanok's gray beach,
With the thousand responsive songs, at random,
My own songs, awaked from that hour,
And with them the key, the word up from the
  waves,
The word of the sweetest song, and all songs,
That strong and delicious word which, creeping to
  my feet,
The sea whispered me.

Elemental Drifts

1

As I ebbed with the ocean of life,
As I wended the shores I know,
As I walked where the sea-ripples wash you,
    Paumanok,
Where they rustle up, hoarse and sibilant,
Where the fierce old mother endlessly cries for her
    castaways,
I, musing, late in the autumn day, gazing off
    southward,
Alone, held by the eternal self of me that threatens
    to get the better of me, and stifle me,
Was seized by the spirit that trails in the lines
    underfoot,
In the rim, the sediment, that stands for all the
    water and all the land of the globe.

Fascinated, my eyes, reverting from the south,
    dropped, to follow those slender windrows,
Chaff, straw, splinters of wood, weeds, and the
    sea-gluten,
Scum, scales from shining rocks, leaves of
    salt-lettuce, left by the tide,
Miles walking, the sound of breaking waves the
    other side of me,
Paumanok, there and then, as I thought the old
    thought of likenesses,
These you presented to me, you fish-shaped island,

As I wended the shores I know,
As I walked with that eternal self of me, seeking
    types.

2
As I wend the shores I know not,
As I listen to the dirge, the voices of men and
    women wrecked,
As I inhale the impalpable breezes that set in
    upon me,
As the ocean so mysterious rolls toward me closer
    and closer,
At once I find, the least thing that belongs to me, or
    that I see or touch, I know not,
I, too, but signify, at the utmost, a little washed-up
    drift,
A few sands and dead leaves to gather,
Gather, and merge, myself as part of the sands and
    drift.

O baffled, balked,
Bent to the very earth, here preceding what follows,
Oppressed with myself that I have dared to open my
    mouth,
Aware now, that, amid all the blab whose echoes
    recoil upon me, I have not once had the least
    idea who or what I am,
But that before all my insolent poems the real
    Me still stands untouched, untold, altogether
    unreached,

Withdrawn far, mocking me with mock-
  congratulatory signs and bows,
With peals of distant ironical laughter at every word
  I have written or shall write,
Striking me with insults till I fall helpless upon the
  sand.

O I perceive I have not understood anything—not
  a single object—and that no man ever can.

I perceive Nature here, in sight of the sea, is taking
  advantage of me, to dart upon me, and sting me,
Because I was assuming so much,
And because I have dared to open my mouth to sing
  at all.

3
You oceans both! You tangible land! Nature!
Be not too rough with me—I submit—I close
  with you,
These little shreds shall, indeed, stand for all.

You friable shore, with trails of debris!
You fish-shaped island! I take what is underfoot,
What is yours is mine, my father.

I too Paumanok,
I too have bubbled up, floated the measureless float,
  and been washed on your shores,
I too am but a trail of drift and debris,

I too leave little wrecks upon you, you fish-shaped
    island.

I throw myself upon your breast, my father,
I cling to you so that you cannot unloose me,
I hold you so firm, till you answer me something.

Kiss me, my father,
Touch me with your lips, as I touch those I love,
Breathe to me, while I hold you close, the secret of
    the wondrous murmuring I envy,
For I fear I shall become crazed, if I cannot emulate
    it, and utter myself as well as it.

Sea-raff! Crook-tongued waves!
O I will yet sing, some day, what you have said
    to me.

4
Ebb, ocean of life, (the flow will return,)
Cease not your moaning, you fierce old mother,
Endlessly cry for your castaways—but fear not, deny
    not me,
Rustle not up so hoarse and angry against my feet,
    as I touch you, or gather from you.

I mean tenderly by you,
I gather for myself, and for this phantom, looking
    down where we lead, and following me and
    mine.

Me and mine!

We, loose windrows, little corpses,

Froth, snowy white, and bubbles,

(See! from my dead lips the ooze exuding at last!

See — the prismatic colors, glistening and rolling!)

Tufts of straw, sands, fragments,

Buoyed hither from many moods, one contradicting
     another,

From the storm, the long calm, the darkness, the
     swell,

Musing, pondering, a breath, a briny tear, a dab of
     liquid or soil,

Up just as much out of fathomless workings
     fermented and thrown,

A limp blossom or two, torn, just as much over waves
     floating, drifted at random,

Just as much for us that sobbing dirge of Nature,

Just as much, whence we come, that blare of the
     cloud-trumpets,

We, capricious, brought hither, we know not
     whence, spread out before you, up there, walking
     or sitting,

Whoever you are — we too lie in drifts at your feet.

Once I Passed Through a Populous City

Once I passed through a populous city, imprinting
     on my brain, for future use, its shows,
     architecture, customs and traditions

But now of all that city I remember only the man
   who wandered with me there, for love of me,
Day by day, and night by night, we were together.
All else has long been forgotten by me—I
   remember, I say, only one rude and ignorant man
   who, when I departed, long and long held me by
   the hand, with silent lips, sad and tremulous.

When I Heard at the Close of the Day

When I heard at the close of the day how my name
   had been received with plaudits in the capitol,
   still it was not a happy night for me that followed,
And else, when I caroused, or when my plans were
   accomplished, still I was not happy,
But the day when I rose at dawn from the bed of
   perfect health, refreshed, singing, inhaling the
   ripe breath of autumn,
When I saw the full moon in the west grow pale and
   disappear in the morning light,
When I wandered alone over the beach, and,
   undressing, bathed, laughing with the cool
   waters, and saw the sun rise,
And when I thought how my dear friend, my lover,
   was on his way coming, O then I was happy,
O then each breath tasted sweeter—and all that day
   my food nourished me more—and the beautiful
   day passed well,

And the next came with equal joy—and with the
next, at evening, came my friend,
And that night, while all was still, I heard the waters
roll slowly continually up the shores,
I heard the hissing rustle of the liquid and sands, as
directed to me, whispering, to congratulate me,
For the one I love most lay sleeping by me under
the same cover in the cool night,
In the stillness, in the autumn moonbeams, his face
was inclined toward me,
And his arm lay lightly around my breast—and that
night I was happy.

A Glimpse

A glimpse, through an interstice caught,
Of a crowd of workmen and drivers in a bar-room,
around the stove, late of a winter night—and I
unremarked, seated in a corner,
Of a youth who loves me, and whom I love, silently
approaching, and seating himself near, that he
may hold me by the hand,
A long while, amid the noises of coming and
going—of drinking and oath and smutty jest,
There we two, content, happy in being together,
speaking little, perhaps not a word.

The Runner

On a flat road runs the well-train'd runner,
He is lean and sinewy, with muscular legs,
He is thinly clothed—he leans forward as he runs,
With lightly closed fists, and arms partially rais'd.

Sparkles from the Wheel

Where the city's ceaseless crowd moves on the
    livelong day,
Withdrawn I join a group of children watching—
    I pause aside with them.

By the curb toward the edge of the flagging,
A knife-grinder works at his wheel sharpening a
    great knife,
Bending over he carefully holds it to the stone—
    by foot and knee,
With measur'd tread he turns rapidly—as he
    presses with light but firm hand,
Forth issue then in copious golden jets,
Sparkles from the wheel.

The scene and all its belongings—how they seize
    and affect me,
The sad sharp-chinn'd old man with worn clothes
    and broad shoulder-band of leather,

Myself effusing and fluid—a phantom curiously
    floating—now here absorb'd and arrested,
The group, (an unminded point set in a vast
    surrounding,)
The attentive, quiet children—the loud, proud,
    restive bass of the streets,
The low hoarse purr of the whirling stone, the
    light-press'd blade,
Diffusing, dropping, sideways-darting, in tiny
    showers of gold,
Sparkles from the wheel.

Bivouac on a Mountain Side

I see before me now, a traveling army halting,
Below, a fertile valley spread, with barns, and the
    orchards of summer,
Behind, the terraced sides of a mountain, abrupt in
    places, rising high,
Broken, with rocks, with clinging cedars, with tall
    shapes, dingily seen,
The numerous camp-fires scatter'd near and far,
    some away up on the mountain,
The shadowy forms of men and horses, looming,
    large-sized, flickering,
And over all, the sky—the sky! far, far out of reach,
    studded with the eternal stars.

Vigil Strange I Kept on the Field One Night

Vigil strange I kept on the field one night,

When you, my son and my comrade, dropt at my
side that day,

One look I but gave, which your dear eyes return'd,
with a look I shall never forget,

One touch of your hand to mine, O boy, reach'd up
as you lay on the ground,

Then onward I sped in the battle, the even-
contested battle,

Till late in the night reliev'd, to the place at last
again I made my way,

Found you in death so cold, dear comrade—found
your body, son of responding kisses, (never again
on earth responding,)

Bared your face in the starlight—curious the
scene—cool blew the moderate night-wind,

Long there and then in vigil I stood, dimly around
me the battle-field spreading,

Vigil wondrous and vigil sweet, there in the fragrant
silent night,

But not a tear fell, not even a long-drawn sigh—
long, long I gazed,

Then on the earth partially reclining, sat by your
side, leaning my chin in my hands,

Passing sweet hours, immortal and mystic hours with
you, dearest comrade—not a tear, not a word,

Vigil of silence, love and death—vigil for you my
son and my soldier,

As onward silently stars aloft, eastward new ones
  upward stole,
Vigil final for you, brave boy, (I could not save you,
  swift was your death,
I faithfully loved you and cared for you living—I
  think we shall surely meet again,)
Till at latest lingering of the night, indeed just as
  the dawn appear'd,
My comrade I wrapt in his blanket, envelop'd well
  his form,
Folded the blanket well, tucking it carefully over
  head, and carefully under feet,
And there and then, and bathed by the rising sun,
  my son in his grave, in his rude-dug grave I
  deposited,
Ending my vigil strange with that—vigil of night
  and battle-field dim,
Vigil for boy of responding kisses, (never again on
  earth responding,)
Vigil for comrade swiftly slain—vigil I never forget,
  how as day brighten'd,
I rose from the chill ground, and folded my soldier
  well in his blanket,
And buried him where he fell.

Reconciliation

Word over all, beautiful as the sky,
Beautiful that war and all its deeds of carnage must
    in time be utterly lost,
That the hands of the sisters Death and Night
    incessantly softly wash again, and ever again, this
    soil'd world;
For my enemy is dead, a man divine as myself is
    dead,
I look where he lies white-faced and still in the
    coffin — I draw near,
Bend down and touch lightly with my lips the white
    face in the coffin.

When Lilacs Last in the Door-yard Bloom'd

1

When lilacs last in the door-yard bloom'd,
And the great star early droop'd in the western sky
    in the night,
I mourn'd — and yet shall mourn with ever-
    returning spring.

O ever-returning spring! trinity sure to me you
    bring,
Lilac blooming perennial, and drooping star in the
    west,
And thought of him I love.

2

O powerful, western, fallen star!

O shades of night! O moody, tearful night!

O great star disappear'd! O the black murk that hides the star!

O cruel hands that hold me powerless! O helpless soul of me!

O harsh surrounding cloud, that will not free my soul!

3

In the door-yard fronting an old farm-house, near the whitewash'd palings,

Stands the lilac bush, tall-growing, with heart-shaped leaves of rich green,

With many a pointed blossom, rising, delicate, with the perfume strong I love,

With every leaf a miracle—and from this bush in the door-yard,

With delicate-color'd blossoms, and heart-shaped leaves of rich green,

A sprig, with its flower, I break.

4

In the swamp, in secluded recesses,

A shy and hidden bird is warbling a song.

Solitary, the thrush,

The hermit, withdrawn to himself, avoiding the settlements,

Sings by himself a song.

Song of the bleeding throat,
Death's outlet song of life—(for well, dear brother,
  I know
If thou wast not gifted to sing, thou would'st surely
  die.)

5

Over the breast of the spring, the land, amid cities,
Amid lanes, and through old woods, (where lately
  the violets peep'd from the ground, spotting the
  gray debris,)
Amid the grass in the fields each side of the lanes—
  passing the endless grass,
Passing the yellow-spear'd wheat, every grain from
  its shroud in the dark-brown fields uprisen,
Passing the apple-tree blows of white and pink in
  the orchards,
Carrying a corpse to where it shall rest in the grave,
Night and day journeys a coffin.

6

Coffin that passes through lanes and streets,
Through day and night, with the great cloud
  darkening the land,
With the pomp of the inloop'd flags, with the cities
  draped in black,
With the show of the States themselves, as of crape-
  veil'd women, standing,
With processions long and winding, and the
  flambeaus of the night,

With the countless torches lit—with the silent sea of
    faces, and the unbared heads,
With the waiting depot, the arriving coffin, and the
    sombre faces,
With dirges through the night, with the thousand
    voices rising strong and solemn,
With all the mournful voices of the dirges, pour'd
    around the coffin,
The dim-lit churches and the shuddering organs—
    where amid these you journey,
With the tolling, tolling bells' perpetual clang,
Here! coffin that slowly passes,
I give you my sprig of lilac.

7

(Nor for you, for one, alone,
Blossoms and branches green to coffins all I bring,
For fresh as the morning—thus would I carol a
    song for you, O sane and sacred death.

All over bouquets of roses,
O death, I cover you over with roses and early
    lilies,
But mostly and now the lilac that blooms the first,
Copious, I break, I break the sprigs from the
    bushes,
With loaded arms I come, pouring for you,
For you, and the coffins all of you, O death.)

8

O western orb, sailing the heaven,

Now I know what you must have meant, as a month
    since we walk'd,

As we walk'd up and down in the dark blue so
    mystic,

As we walk'd in silence the transparent shadowy
    night,

As I saw you had something to tell, as you bent to
    me night after night,

As you droop'd from the sky low down, as if to my
    side, (while the other stars all look'd on,)

As we wander'd together the solemn night, (for
    something, I know not what, kept me from
    sleep,)

As the night advanced, and I saw on the rim of the
    west, ere you went, how full you were of woe,

As I stood on the rising ground in the breeze, in the
    cold transparent night,

As I watch'd where you pass'd and was lost in the
    netherward black of the night,

As my soul, in its trouble, dissatisfied, sank, as where
    you, sad orb,

Concluded, dropt in the night, and was gone.

9

Sing on, there in the swamp!

O singer bashful and tender! I hear your notes—
    I hear your call,

I hear—I come presently—I understand you,
But a moment I linger—for the lustrous star has
    detain'd me,
The star, my comrade departing, holds and
    detains me.

10

O how shall I warble myself for the dead one there
    I loved?
And how shall I deck my song for the large sweet
    soul that has gone?
And what shall my perfume be, for the grave of him
    I love?

Sea-winds, blown from east and west,
Blown from the eastern sea, and blown from the
    western sea, till there on the prairies meeting,
These, and with these, and the breath of my chant,
I perfume the grave of him I love.

11

O what shall I hang on the chamber walls?
And what shall the pictures be that I hang on the
    walls,
To adorn the burial-house of him I love?

Pictures of growing spring, and farms, and homes,
With the Fourth-month eve at sundown, and the
    gray smoke lucid and bright,

With floods of the yellow gold of the gorgeous,
  indolent, sinking sun, burning, expanding
  the air,
With the fresh sweet herbage under foot, and the
  pale green leaves of the trees prolific,
In the distance the flowing glaze, the breast of the
  river, with a wind-dapple here and there,
With ranging hills on the banks, with many a line
  against the sky, and shadows,
And the city at hand, with dwellings so dense, and
  stacks of chimneys,
And all the scenes of life, and the workshops, and
  the workmen homeward returning.

12

Lo! body and soul! this land!
Mighty Manhattan, with spires, and the sparkling
  and hurrying tides, and the ships,
The varied and ample land—the South and the
  North in the light—Ohio's shores, and flashing
  Missouri,
And ever the far-spreading prairies, cover'd with
  grass and corn.

Lo! the most excellent sun, so calm and haughty,
The violet and purple morn, with just-felt breezes,
The gentle, soft-born, measureless light,
The miracle, spreading, bathing all—the fulfill'd
  noon,

The coming eve, delicious—the welcome night,
and the stars,
Over my cities shining all, enveloping man and
land.

13

Sing on! sing on, you gray-brown bird!
Sing from the swamps, the recesses—pour your
chant from the bushes,
Limitless out of the dusk, out of the cedars and
pines.

Sing on, dearest brother—warble your reedy song,
Loud human song, with voice of uttermost woe.

O liquid, and free, and tender!
O wild and loose to my soul—O wondrous singer!
You only I hear—yet the star holds me, (but will
soon depart,)
Yet the lilac, with mastering odor, holds me.

14

Now while I sat in the day, and look'd forth,
In the close of the day, with its light, and the fields
of spring, and the farmer preparing his crops,
In the large unconscious scenery of my land, with its
lakes and forests,
In the heavenly aerial beauty, (after the perturb'd
winds, and the storms,)

Under the arching heavens of the afternoon
 swift passing, and the voices of children and
 women,
The many-moving sea-tides,—and I saw the ships
 how they sail'd,
And the summer approaching with richness, and
 the fields all busy with labor,
And the infinite separate houses, how they all went
 on, each with its meals and minutia of daily
 usages,
And the streets, how their throbbings throbb'd,
 and the cities pent—lo! then and there,
Falling among them all, and upon them all,
 enveloping me with the rest,
Appear'd the cloud, appear'd the long black trail,
And I knew death, its thought, and the sacred
 knowledge of death.

Then with the knowledge of death as walking one
 side of me,
And the thought of death close-walking the other
 side of me,
And I in the middle, as with companions, and as
 holding the hands of companions,
I fled forth to the hiding receiving night, that
 talks not,
Down to the shores of the water, the path by the
 swamp in the dimness,
To the solemn shadowy cedars, and ghostly pines
 so still.

And the singer so shy to the rest receiv'd me,
The gray-brown bird I know, receiv'd us comrades
three,
And he sang what seem'd the song of death, and a
verse for him I love.

From deep secluded recesses,
From the fragrant cedars, and the ghostly pines so
still,
Came the singing of the bird.

And the charm of the singing rapt me,
As I held, as if by their hands, my comrades in the
night,
And the voice of my spirit tallied the song of the
bird.

Come, lovely and soothing death,
Undulate round the world, serenely arriving, arriving,
In the day, in the night, to all, to each,
Sooner or later, delicate death.

Prais'd be the fathomless universe,
For life and joy, and for objects and knowledge curious,
And for love, sweet love—but praise! O praise and praise!
For the sure-enwinding arms of cool-enfolding death.

Dark mother, always gliding near, with soft feet,
Have none chanted for thee a chant of fullest welcome?
Then I chant it for thee—I glorify thee above all,

I bring thee a song that when thou must indeed come, come
*   unfalteringly.*

Approach, strong deliveress!
When it is so—when thou hast taken them, I joyously sing
*   the dead,*
Lost in the loving, floating ocean of thee,
Laved in the flood of thy bliss, O death.

From me to thee glad serenades,
Dances for thee I propose, saluting thee—adornments and
*   feastings for thee,*
And the sights of the open landscape, and the high-spread
*   sky, are fitting,*
And life and the fields, and the huge and thoughtful
*   night.*

The night, in silence, under many a star,
The ocean shore, and the husky whispering wave, whose
*   voice I know,*
And the soul turning to thee, O vast and well-veil'd
*   death,*
And the body gratefully nestling close to thee.

Over the tree-tops I float thee a song!
Over the rising and sinking waves—over the myriad
*   fields, and the prairies wide,*
Over the dense-pack'd cities all, and the teeming wharves
*   and ways,*
I float this carol with joy, with joy to thee, O death!

15

To the tally of my soul,
Loud and strong kept up the gray-brown bird,
With pure, deliberate notes, spreading, filling the
    night.

Loud in the pines and cedars dim,
Clear in the freshness moist, and the swamp-
    perfume,
And I with my comrades there in the night.

While my sight that was bound in my eyes unclosed,
As to long panoramas of visions.

And I saw askant the armies,
I saw, as in noiseless dreams, hundreds of battle-
    flags,
Borne through the smoke of the battles, and pierc'd
    with missiles, I saw them,
And carried hither and yon through the smoke, and
    torn and bloody,
And at last but a few shreds left on the staffs, (and
    all in silence,)
And the staffs all splinter'd and broken.

I saw battle-corpses, myriads of them,
And the white skeletons of young men—I saw them,
I saw the debris and debris of all the dead soldiers
    of the war,
But I saw they were not as was thought,

They themselves were fully at rest—they suffer'd
    not,
The living remain'd and suffer'd—the mother
    suffer'd,
And the wife and the child, and the musing
    comrade suffer'd,
And the armies that remain'd suffer'd.

16

Passing the visions, passing the night,
Passing, unloosing the hold of my comrades' hands,
Passing the song of the hermit bird, and the tallying
    song of my soul,
Victorious song, death's outlet song, yet varying,
    ever-altering song,
As low and wailing, yet clear the notes, rising and
    falling, flooding the night,
Sadly sinking and fainting, as warning and warning,
    and yet again bursting with joy,
Covering the earth, and filling the spread of the
    heaven,
As that powerful psalm in the night I heard from
    recesses,
Must I leave thee, lilac with heart-shaped leaves,
Must I leave thee there in the door-yard, blooming,
    returning with spring,
Must I pass from my song for thee,
From my gaze on thee in the west, fronting the west,
    communing with thee,
O comrade lustrous, with silver face in the night.

Yet each I keep, and all, retrievements out of the
  night,
The song, the wondrous chant of the gray-brown
  bird I keep,
And the tallying chant, the echo arous'd in my soul
  I keep,
With the lustrous and drooping star, with the
  countenance full of woe,
With the lilac tall, and its blossoms of mastering
  odor,
With the holders holding my hand, nearing the call
  of the bird,
Comrades mine, and I in the midst, and their
  memory ever I keep—for the dead I loved so
  well,
For the sweetest, wisest soul of all my days and
  lands—and this for his dear sake;
Lilac and star and bird, twined with the chant of my
  soul,
There in the fragrant pines, and the cedars dusk
  and dim.

The Last Invocation

At the last, tenderly,
From the walls of the powerful fortress'd house,
From the clasp of the knitted locks, from the keep
  of the well-closed doors,
Let me be wafted.

Let me glide noiselessly forth;
With the key of softness unlock the locks—with a
    whisper,
Set ope the doors O soul.

Tenderly—be not impatient,
(Strong is your hold O mortal flesh,
Strong is your hold O love.)

ABOUT THE TEXT

Following the title of each poem are the date of the version used in this book; the other titles, if any, under which it appeared; and the section and line numbers where readings from other versions have been incorporated (except when these are limited to punctuation, spelling, and lineation).

Song of Myself: A Poem of Walt Whitman, an American 1855 (1855: without title; 1856: *A Poem of Walt Whitman, an American;* 1860: *Walt Whitman;* 1881: *Song of Myself*) **3.** Line 9: 1856. **5.** Lines 6 and 7: 1860; line 10: 1867; line 12: 1856. **7.** Line after line 14, dropped: 1867. **8.** Line 9: 1856. **15.** Line after line 27, dropped: 1867. **17.** Line after line 2, dropped: 1867. **24.** Line 31: 1867. **32.** Line 8: 1881. **33.** Line 69: 1860. **37.** Line 2: 1860; seven lines after line 2 and two lines after last line, dropped: 1867. **42.** Line 7: 1856. **46.** Line 8: 1860; line 9: 1881; lines 22 and 27: 1867. **51.** Line 3: 1881.

Sleep-Chasings 1855 (1855: without title; 1856: *Night Poem;* 1860: with this title; 1871: *The Sleepers*) **1.** Lines 65 and 66: 1856. **8.** Two lines after last line, dropped: 1856.

Poem of the Body 1881 (1855: without title; 1856: with this title; 1867: *I Sing the Body Electric*) **1.** Lines 3 and 4: 1856. **2.** Lines 16 and 20: 1856. **5.** Line after last line, dropped: 1860. **6.** Line 14: 1881; lines 15 and 17: 1860. **7.** Line 7: 1856. **9.** Entire section added: 1856; line 2: 1860.

There Was a Child Went Forth 1855 (1855: without title; 1856: *Poem of the Child That Went Forth, and Always Goes Forth, Forever and Forever;* 1871: with this title) Line 2: 1867. Line after last line, dropped: 1867.

Crossing Brooklyn Ferry 1881 (1856: *Sun-Down Poem;* 1860: with this title) **6.** Line 10: 1856. **9.** Line 7: 1856.

Poem of the Proposition of Nakedness 1856 (1856: with this title; 1867: *Respondez!;* excluded from *Leaves of Grass:* 1881) Lines 2 and 3: 1871. Line 4: 1860. Line 11: 1871. Line 27: 1860. Lines 35, 50, 58, and 59: 1871.

Out of the Cradle Endlessly Rocking 1860 (1860: *A Word Out of the Sea;* 1871: with this title) Line 1: 1871. Line after line 2, dropped: 1867. Line 24: 1871.

Elemental Drifts 1860 (1860: without title; 1867: with this title; 1881: *As I Ebbed with the Ocean of Life*) Two lines before first line, dropped: 1881.

Once I Passed Through a Populous City, undated (Manuscript: without title; 1860: without title; 1867: with this title).

When I Heard at the Close of the Day 1860 (1860: without title; 1867: with this title).

A Glimpse 1867 (1860: without title).

The Runner 1867.

Sparkles from the Wheel 1871.

Bivouac on a Mountain Side 1865.

Vigil Strange I Kept on the Field One Night 1865.

Reconciliation 1881.

When Lilacs Last in the Door-yard Bloom'd 1865–6
5. Line 4: 1881; **14.** Line 40: 1871; **15.** Lines 9 and 10: 1881; lines 13 and 17: 1871; **16.** Line 14: 1871; line 19: 1871; line after line 22, dropped: 1871.

The Last Invocation (1871).